Pharaoh's Wife

Pharaoh's Wife
An Occult Novel

by
Félicien Champsaur

translated, annotated and introduced by
Brian Stableford

A Black Coat Press Book

ISBN 978-1-61227-156-9. First Printing. March 2013. Published by Black Coat Press, an imprint of Hollywood Comics.com, LLC, P.O. Box 17270, Encino, CA 91416. All rights reserved. Except for review purposes, no part of this book may be reproduced or transmitted in any form or by any means, electronic or mechanical, including photocopying, recording, or by any information storage and retrieval system, without permission in writing from the publisher. The stories and characters depicted in this novel are entirely fictional. Printed in the United States of America.

Introduction

La Pharaonne, roman occulte by Félicien Champsaur, here translated as *Pharaoh's Wife: An Occult Novel*, was originally published in Paris in 1929 by Ferenczi et fils, illustrated by an "archaeological commentary" designed by the Italian artist Fabius Lorenzi. It is an odd book, perhaps because it appears to have been written "backwards." If the evidence of the text can be trusted, the author must have undertaken a voyage to Egypt early in 1928, traveling up the Nile over a period of weeks, making elaborate notes of his observations for future reference. Wanting to make use of that material in a novel, he then appears to have designed a long prelude establishing the characters that would, so to speak, take his place in the story as observers of what he had seen, his notes providing the raw material for the journey that would take them toward the climax of their own story.

Not unnaturally—like Champsaur's own expedition, presumably—the story he concocted in order to make use of his notes on Egypt was inspired by the discovery of the nearly-intact tomb of Tutankhamun by Howard Carter and the Earl of Carnarvon in November 1922, which caused a sensation and renewed worldwide interest in Egyptian archeology and Egyptian tourism. The tomb's burial chamber was opened in February 1923, and Carnarvon's death not long after helped to fuel yellow press stories about a supposed "curse of the mummy's tomb"—an idea already familiar thanks to sensational silent movies, most notably *Die Angen deer Mummir Ma* (1918; English version as *The Eyes of the*

Mummy) directed by Ernst Lubitsch and starring Pola Negri. That notion, however, was merely an understandable extrapolation of the intrinsic fascination and essential eccentricity of the burial practices of ancient Egypt. The idea of mummification, summoned from the imagination of the ancient Egyptians to provide the foundation of a bizarre cult built around the nucleus of a curious immortality, inevitably found an echo in the imagination of the modern audience aware of the mass exhumation of mummies through the medium of press reportage.

Champsaur's contemplation of Lord Carnarvon's discovery was inevitably complicated by nationalistic considerations. The first wave of Egyptian archeological explorations had been carried out by French scholars in the wake of Napoléon Bonaparte's Egyptian campaign, and Egyptology had been a French-based science for most of the 19th century—but the French explorers who had excavated so much had failed to find the Tutankhamun tomb, the most nearly complete of all the Pharaonic tombs—which having only been robbed once in antiquity, by thieves who had been careful enough to hide their find after removing the jewelry, but apparently not careful enough to stay alive long enough to return. That had been left for the English, who became the masters of Egypt after the Great War, to discover—a circumstance bound to cause a certain faint resentment in Paris.

It had also been in France that writers associated with the Romantic Movement had made the most productive use of the romance of ancient Egypt, and, more specifically, the romance of mummification, in their writings. Théophile Gautier penned "Le Pied de Momie" (1840; tr. as "The Mummy's Foot") and *Le Roman de la Momie* (1858; tr. as *The Romance of a Mummy*) as well as his classic account of "Une Nuit de Cléopâtre" (1838; tr. as "One of Cleopatra's Nights"). The romance in question was, however, already tinged with irony, and a certain amount of disillusionment, the latter very evident in Joseph Méry's "Les Explorations de Victor Hummer" (1836; tr. as "The Explorations of Victor Hummer"[1]), a work that has a considerable kinship with *La Pharaonne*.

That literary baton was also passed on, however, when the notion that mummies might retain, or at least recover, a strange form of life became a rich aliment for popular fiction produced in association with the 19th century "occult revival," particularly in association with romances of reincarnation, which dealt with historical recurrences occasioned by reincarnation, and quests for love extended across millennia. The greatest success of the subgenre in question, H. Rider Haggard's *She* (1886), only had a peripheral Egyptian element, but Haggard wrote similar novels moving ancient Egypt to center stage, as did several of his English contemporaries. Haggard's own account of *Cleopatra* (1889) is a fairly straightforward historical fantasy, but Cleopatra and earlier queens of Egypt such as Nefertiti soon began to take a central role in English literary fantasies of reincarnation, both fictional and delusional. The entire apparatus was carried forward into the lurid depths of cheap popular fiction—notably by "Sax Rohmer" (Arthur Sarsfield Ward), whose Egyptian fantasies of real or apparent reincarnation included *Brood of the Witch-Queen* (1918) and *She Who Sleeps* (1928)—and, of course, into silent movies.

---

[1] Included in the Black Coat Press edition of *The Tower of Destiny*, ISBN 978-1-61227-101-9.

The occult revival ran out of steam at the end of the century, but never faded away entirely, and received a further boost as a result of the Great War, when some of its components—most notably spiritualism— experienced a renewal of popularity born of grief and widespread disillusionment with the science and tech- nology that had not only made the conflict of 1914-18 so bloody but promised far worse for the next clash of na- tions. It was in that historical context that the discovery of Tutankhamun's tomb sparked a new popular interest in ancient Egypt in general and mummies in particular.

Attitudes had shifted very markedly since the 1880s, and romances of reincarnation produced in the 1920s had to partake of a new zeitgeist as well as their modern dimension having to be painted against a very different historical backcloth. Commitment of any kind of belief had become much harder, and analysis of that kind of commitment much more confused. Champsaur, who had always been a skeptic unsure of whether there was anything in which a rational man could pin his faith, and equally unsure as to what the lest worst alternative might be in the matter of making do, but had always been simultaneously entranced by the possibility of in- tellectual and spiritual progress, was as well-placed as anyone, if not to find any answer to the conundrums re- excited by the spectacular discovery of Tutankhamun's tomb, at least to exemplify the groping in the dark that seemed to be the intellectual and imaginative plight of the post-war decade.[2]

_____

[2] A more detailed account of Champsaur's career can be found in the introduction to the Black Coat Press edition of *The Hu- man Arrow* (2011; tr. of *Les Ailes de l'homme*), ISBN 978-1- 61227-045-6.

To some readers, *La Pharaonne* must have seemed a disappointment, because of its querulous rambling as well as it interruption by a limping travelogue, and it might have come to seem that way to its author too. Champsaur obviously made the story up as he went along, as was his usual practice, and his uncertainty as to where he wanted to take it led to several significant inconsistencies as well as to numerous introductions of minor characters who were then unceremoniously abandoned and forgotten. The inevitably patchiness of the travelogue, which is a disconnected series of holiday snapshots devoid of any narrative traction save for the itinerary of the journey, is curiously reflected in the story devised to frame it, which is also a rather loose aggregation of separate images and scenes, distinct and sometimes flamboyant in themselves, but with such limited little overall coherency that the whole bears more resemblance to a literary collage than an organized narrative. That effect is not without its own artistry, however, and its sheer idiosyncrasy provides some compensation for a lack of efficient steering that it certainly not out of keeping with the zeitgeist it reflects.

In spite of its uncertainties, Champsaur's improvised plot is possessed of a zest typical of the author's endeavors, and the disconnection of its parts leaves room not only for the casual philosophical flights of fancy in which he loved to indulge—which are particularly abundant here—but also for some eccentric digressions. Never a writer afraid of self-indulgence, Champsaur evidently reveled in that opportunity, and the hectic confusion of his digressions has a certain unique charm. At any rate, the various dead ends strewn around the prologue do not provide any significant delay, and the inevitable languors of the travelogue are not sufficiently extended to become truly tedious. One can easily imagine that looking at Champaur's actual holiday snaps would be as unexciting as looking at anyone else's, but that the wit and enthusiasm of his commentary would probably have provided adequate compensation.

In any case, Champsaur appears to have come to the conclusion of his own accord that his insertion of the travelogue into his novel had brought his plot to an inconvenient standstill, and to have become bored with the procrastination himself. Eventually, he brings his reminiscence to an abrupt halt, in order to return at a headlong rush to his story. Once resumed, even the story had nowhere to go—but that, in a sense, was the whole point of the exercise. Even if, as the narrative seems prepared to accept—albeit a trifle reluctantly—there is some reliability in occultism, and some underlying truth in the notion of serial reincarnation, so what? What further conclusion can possibly be reached or drawn, except that there are more things in Heaven and Earth that are dreamt of in flapper philosophy? And again, so what?

It is arguable, in fact, that the most intriguing element of Champsaur's narrative scheme is not the possibility that its heroine really is, in some sense, the Pharaoh Tutankhamun's wife, or even the psychological effects that the belief in question might have on her attempt to find a purpose in life. Champsaur obviously intended that to be the principal focus of his story when he set out, but he and the story got sidetracked along the way, as he became more intrigued by the other set of echoes of the past that he had deftly set up by way of comparison and contrast: the entirely mundane but nevertheless forceful burdens of association that weigh upon the Duke of Rutland and his amiable parasite William Shakespeare, eccentrically bonded together by the admittedly-false theory that the original William Shakespeare's plays might really have been written by Roger Manners, Earl of Rutland.

Although initially invoked as mere comedy relief, only emerging tentatively from the wings of the romance of reincarnation, the Duke and Shakespeare are ultimately set free to hog the stage. Although remaining conscientiously farcical, their subplot gradually becomes more poignant in its tragic dimension, in spite of, and partly because of, its frank absurdity. Members of a supplementary cast they might be, in terms of the novel's central theme, but the story acquires a more abundant life whenever Rutland and Shakespeare take the stage away from the Duchess and Ormus, and they have all its best lines, in spite of sterling competition from the likes of Charlie Chaplin and King Fuad I of Egypt, whose mere appearance in the plot is enough to cause starts of surprise.

As is inevitable with a novel published in 1929, *La Pharaonne* has dated considerably. We now know far more about Tutankhamun than it was possible for Champsaur and his characters to know or guess in 1929. Tutankhamun's sarcophagus was not opened in order to expose the mummy of the king until October 1925, and the tomb had not yet been fully emptied of its contents when Champsaur visited Egypt and wrote the novel. Although Tutankhamun had not previously attracted much attention from Egyptologists, it was known that he had died young—which had inevitably gave rise to speculation that he had been murdered, perhaps by poison—and news relating to discoveries made in the tomb and by the study of its contents was filtered through that knowledge, but it was not until much later that the king's precise age was revealed, along with his actual parentage, and many other details of his brief career were filled in.

It is therefore entirely excusable that the account of Tutankhamun's life that Champsaur puts into Ormus' mouth has subsequently been revealed to be false in almost every respect, and that the overall historical context provided by Adsum is similarly unsupportable. It is obvious, however, that when Champsaur first began developing those schemes he had not yet made up his mind whether the story of Tutanhkamun and the more general account of Egyptian religion offered by Ormus and Adsum were to be anything more than a line of patter developed by two charlatans, albeit charlatans who had fallen—as charlatans often do—for their own propaganda, so his blithe carelessness is understandable. In any case, there is no reason why our knowledge of the fantasy's falsehood should undermine its interest as an aspect of the novel, either as a mere flight of fancy, or as a hypothetical psychological lever.

As a result of all the problems cited above, aficionados of supernatural fiction might find *La Pharaonne* a trifle half-hearted, and deem it weak in consequence, but true connoisseurs will observe that its hesitations and uncertainties allow it to address more subtle questions than any that Rider Haggard was able to reach, let alone Sax Rohmer, and to investigate them more delicately, if more than a little casually. Like almost all of Champsaur's fiction, *La Pharaonne* is primarily a love story, and it reflects the author's genuine interest in the deceptive and treacherous appeals of that emotion, and the essential perversity of its efforts toward the ideal, as well as the essential hollowness of any attempt to avoid or sacrifice its ideality. It is not his strongest story of that sort, nor even his most endearingly peculiar,[3] but it is one of his more adventurous, in a spirit of open-minded exploration, and hence one of the most interesting.

This translation has been made from the version of the Ferenczi edition reproduced on the Bibliothèque Nationale's *gallica* website. The translation was unusually difficult because of the text's eccentric way with proper names. The frank and deliberate bizarrerie of many of the names attached to minor American and English characters is further confused by variations in their rendering; I have unified them as best I could. More seriously, the names attached to places and natural species are subject to similar variation, and often seem to be erratic or erroneous—perhaps because the notes that Champsaur made while he was in Egypt routinely guessed at the spelling of words he heard spoken, with results that cannot be located in other texts, and often made different guesses on different occasions. Other mistakes in the text might well result from the typesetter's inability to read Champsaur's handwriting and a lack of conscientious proofreading.

At any rate, there are a great many puzzling manifestations in the French text that do not lend themselves to easy interpretation or confident correction. I have made corrections where I could, and substituted versions of some of the names that are more likely to be recognized by modern readers, but for the most part I have simply followed the policy of reproducing names as they are given in the French text, even when they are un-

---

[3] The latter distinction surely belongs to *Ouha, roi des singes* (1923; tr. as *Ouha, King of the Apes*), Black Coat Press, ISBN 978-1-61227-115-6.

known to authoritative geography or natural history, only adding footnotes to a handful of the most problematic cases.

Brian Stableford

PART ONE: ORMUS' INCANTATION

I. The Mage Ormus

After the stifling heat of summer, the month of September is perhaps the one, in New York, whose weather is the most disconcerting. In winter, the temperature sometimes descends as far as twenty degrees below zero, while in summer one is positively grilled there. In July and August the dwellings are no longer habitable, and the unfortunate citizens sleep in parks and on the roofs of their buildings. September and October finally become tolerable—the two most agreeable months of the year in Fifth Avenue, where the billionaires of a city constructed for commercial and financial establishments have their splendid town houses.

From Brooklyn Bridge, which overlooks the city from its forty-meter height, eyes considering New York by day see nothing but a mass of brick and iron buildings, in which the skyscrapers look like enormous towers—but at night, the décor changes. Among millions of electrically-lighted windows, the strings of high street-lights in the avenues, intersecting at right-angles, design an enormous sparkling chessboard of stars. Mirrored in the river, the formidable bridge, two kilometers long and twenty-six meters wide, with its eight tracks for trains and trams, two roads for automobiles and a pedestrian footpath, is brilliantly illuminated, in flowing streaks of fire endlessly repeated by the water, resembling a fairy-land of light.

While everywhere else in the city is feverishly crowded and agitated, Fifth Avenue enjoys a relative calm, an oasis in the movement of business and unrelenting work. The façades of the big houses have a rich and monumental appearance, but that is not where there is life and movement. The real luxury and intimate life is hidden behind then; it is in the gardens that everything is disposed for the pleasure of the inhabitants. The most opulent are, in any case, not content with these splendid dwellings; on Long Island, the large isle that borders the Atlantic outside New York, there are veritable palaces whose grounds strive to outdo Versailles.

Such was the case with Diana, Duchess of Rutland, who, in addition to her magnificent house in Fifth Avenue, had a mansion on the island whose magnificence and comfort eclipsed the most beautiful properties of the Old World.

Diana Bering, the daughter of the billionaire Nathan Bering, a king of Industry, had been able to satisfy her every desire and whim since early childhood. After a very complete education she had entered social life at the age of eighteen. Diana's colossal fortune put her beyond compare, but the daughters of plutocrats are not much sought-after by Yankees. It being usual in the United States not to provide daughters with dowries, dollar millionaires marry for love; they espouse young women who, if not poor, are at least less well-off than they are, rather than heiresses whose wealth overshadows their own. Because of that, a certain number of more fortunate young women remain spinsters, or fall back on the nobility of old Europe, where they also find a satisfaction of their vanity. It was thus that Diana Bering had become the Duchess of Rutland.

The Duke, an English gentleman, bore one of the oldest British names; there had been a Rutland in the reign of Richard II, which is to say, around 1400: Duke Aumerle of Rutland, the son of the Duke of York.[4] The Duke had an illustrious name, and also debts of four million, which Nathan Bering paid in full. Once married, Diana led the life she wanted, traveling alone or with her husband. More often, she was alone; Rutland would have been considered absolutely lacking in good taste had he not let the Duchess do as she wished. The latter, for her part, scarcely paid any heed to her husband, who enjoyed the same liberty. It was, therefore, a society marriage of the best kind, and never, in the twelve years that it had been contracted, had the slightest cloud appeared in the sky of the two spouses' bed, each of them having had the tact not to be too attached to it.

In her adolescence, Diana, like all girls, had followed the program of physical education practiced in the New World. Scarcely sensual then, her amorous fantasies had been rare. The Duke had certainly not had the same temperament, but in the United States, gallant life is rather limited. It required the Great War for male youth to acquire a taste for pleasure in Europe and bring back more dissolute mores.

---

[4] The Duke of Rutland is a real English title and was in use when Champsaur wrote the novel; if the ninth duke, John Henry Montagu Manners (1886-1940), was aware of his fictional counterpart he evidently made no complaint. The additional title created for Edward of Norwich, Duke of Aumerle by Richard II was actually Earl of Rutland, but that title fell into disuse after his death until its recreation in the 16th century, when it became the prerogative of the Manners family.

When she was not traveling—and she traveled a great deal, having two yachts and a number of automobiles—the Duchess lived in her mansion on Long Island, Redge House. On the fifth of September 1927, however, she had gone to New York, attracted by the arrival in the city of the Mage Ormus, who was all the rage among the city's female population—and in her small drawing-room with authentic Louis XV furniture, there were five pretty female visitors in animated conversation with the Duchess.

"The Mage is astonishing," said Ame Love, the daughter of Mordant Love. For one thing, he's too handsome. He reminds me of a god. A contemporary of anterior lives, which he remembers, he talks about the past with a disconcerting authority."

"Has he been in New York long?" asked the Duchess.

"Only three weeks. It's Countess Olivani-Sforza who knew him. It was at her house that I saw him for the first time, four days ago. He's an amazing thought-reader."

"Really?" exclaimed Betty Herald, a magnificent blonde, the wife of the celebrated engineering genius Pall Herald, the constructor of the Great Lakes ferry. "What was he able to tell you? I didn't think you were very sensitive to suggestion."

"I'd like to see you resist, when his great yellow eyes stare you in the face."

"And he told you what you were thinking?"

"Exactly—me and the others."

"It's diabolical," said Mary O'Brien, crossing herself. She was an extremely Catholic Irishwoman who lived in Diana's house. "This Ormus is an incarnation of the Evil Spirit."

"Shut up, Mary," said the Duchess. "You're being silly, my dear."

Her situation in Diana's house put Mary O'Brien completely under the Duchess's domination, and in spite of her revolutionary spirit, the Irishwoman, an exile without resources, was obliged to submit to her meekly. She dared not make any reply.

Mary was a very unusual individual: the last descendant of a family of Irish patriots, her extreme feminism had, in a way, had her ostracized from all the small political groups, and since Ireland had become independent she had left the country in order to travel the world preaching female emancipation. Unfortunately, she had no money and could only support herself on the fruits of her efforts, political pamphlets bringing in very little and lectures not much more. She had been lucky enough to meet Diana in Canada. The latter had been enthused by the young evangelist's ideas, had offered her a refuge in her home and gave her funds for an active propaganda.

Mary was a tall, thin woman twenty-five years of age, with strongly-accentuated masculine features, black hair cut very short, a round face, and keen and luminous eyes. Her great charm was her clear, definite and seductive voice. The five women visiting Diana were all converts to her cause and gave her the aid of their considerable influence—and the five women gathered at that moment in the Duchess of Rutland's home were incontestably among the richest and most beautiful in America.

The Duchess was in the splendor of maturity. Tall and admirably composed, only a slight creasing in the corners of her eyes denounced the wrinkles to come. Bright chestnut-colored hair framed a face slightly sun-bronzed by habitual traveling, firm and full and a trifle highly-colored, illuminated by magnificent jet-black eyes.

By contrast, Ame Love was a dainty blonde; her hair surrounded her face, like that of a little eighteenth-century doll, with a fleecy cloud. Her eyes were periwinkle blue. She was as lively as a bird, a delicate little thing, a Greuze of the prettiest sort.[5]

Kate Souvermann, the daughter of the multimillionaire Karl Souvermann, the director of the Old Silver Bank, retained from her German origins the slightly exaggerated plenitude of the daughters of that nation, but she was certainly one of its finest specimens. Tall, with superb arms and shoulders, perhaps a little too muscular, but very pale, blue eyes, and a complexion, not of lilies and roses but strawberries and cream, she had a beauty that created an appetite—for kisses and caresses, that is.

Betty Herald was a very American beauty: sturdy, molded in the flesh of a Greek goddess, coiffed in bronze-red, with fiery green eyes beneath her marble forehead. Athletic, skilled in all sports, she was capable of carrying her husband, the engineer of the Great Lakes, with her arms at full stretch.

The Margrave Oswald von Weringen was also a pure-blooded American, but from the South, born in New Orleans. She had the litheness of her native land and a Spanish slenderness, with profound dark eyes and dark hair that almost had a tint of blue. Always smiling, amiable and cordial, one sensed a pure descendant of the Latin race in her. She had married Von Weringen, a Viennese resident in North America for twenty years,

---

[5] The painter Jean-Baptiste Greuze (1725-1805) was famous for sentimental family scenes and rather sickly portraits.

initially as a Klondike gold-prospector; he had founded a fur company with the precious metal recovered from placers, which had made him a millionaire several times over, and he was still working. At present, he had a monopoly on all the large reserves of furs and was centralizing his stocks.

The conversation continued.

"Mary's not entirely wrong," said Ame Love. "A man like that scares me. Anything out of the ordinary makes me shiver. Isn't it enough to live our lives?"

What's the point of living," Kate, exclaimed, "if we can't understand the enigma of life? Do we have an afterlife? That would be interesting to know. Must we disappear without that hope?"

"Kate's right," said Diana. "Have we arrived at the summit of civilization only for our intelligence to expire like a blown-out match? Is that possible? So, I'm passionate about everything that touches on matters of the beyond. There's an impenetrable mystery in death, and it's necessary to search for the key by any means possible. I want to see this Mage Ormus."

"He'll astonish you," said Ame Love. "He didn't say a word about the future life, but for the transmigration of souls in the past he's astonishing. Listen to this! People were talking about the excavations undertaken in Egypt by Lord Carnarvon, and he smiled ironically. 'Lord Carnarvon,' he said, 'was on the wrong track. The tombs he excavated had already been visited. In 942 B.C.—which is to say, in 4223 of the Memphic era, I was a servant of a priest of Helios[6] named Phi-Zouma.

---

[6] Helios was, of course, a Greek sun god, but French writers of the 19th and early 20th centuries often used Greek names for their "equivalent" Egyptian gods—as, of course, the Greeks

Hating the rites of the priests of Amon, he took a malign pleasure—which was also very fruitful—in excavating and robbing the tombs erected under the old religion. It was at his instigation, and on his orders, that I, the humble Levite Omsrah, visited the tomb excavated by Lord Carnarvon five thousand years ago. I can, in consequence, assure you that he has only found what I left for him to find.'

"'You've lived in those fabulous epochs, then?' I asked. 'Life then must have had a grandeur and a majesty far above that of our vulgar epoch?'

"'That depends on the manner in which one understands human existence and antiquity,' Ormus replied. 'The Pharaoh was forced, in public life, always to maintain a hieratic attitude and a grandiose appearance, making him seem like a god to the populace—immobile, his eyes fixed in an impassive stare, indifferently—which demanded an attitude and behavior that had nothing agreeable about it for the sovereign. We priests, who were the principal scene-dressers of those absolute despots, were able to laugh at them in private. Worshipers of Helios, we were scornful of those fanatical idolaters, the priests of Amon,[7] who, after having banished our

---

had when they ruled Egypt; thus the Greeks named an important Egyptian city Heliopolis because it seemed to have been the center of worship of the Egyptian sun god, usually known as Amon-Ra or Amun-Re.

[7] Whether accidentally or deliberately, Ormus appears to be confusing Amon/Amun, who was the equivalent of Helios, with Aten, whose worship displaced that of Amun-Re for a while during the eighteenth dynasty. Both were sun gods, but the one whose monotheistic worship was instituted by the Pharaoh Akhenaten was his personal deity. Osiris, on the other hand, was not a sun god at all but the god of the afterlife. Ak-

master Osiris, had instituted the cult of Pharaoh as man and god by means of base flattery. But away from the external pomp, he became simply human again. How many times have I heard Pharaoh Amaris III, who was then our sovereign, laughing and joking with Phi-Zouma, and even, with me, the poor Levite? He was only a man then, and very glad to dispose of his mask of quasi-divinity.'

"'It's necessary to conserve our illusions,' someone put in. 'I picture the men of ancient Egypt in accordance the scale and grandeur of their monuments.'

"'They had the nobility, at least, if not the height,' the Mage replied. 'The costumes and traditions of that epoch imposed a certain majesty of gesture and language.'

"Then, for more than an hour, ladies, Ormus told us mummified anecdotes, like memories of yesterday, describing the customs of very remote times in the manner of a man who had lived in them—times so ancient that they've fallen into eternal dust."

A man had come into the room a few moments before, and, in order not to interrupt the speaker, had remained near the door. He came forward and bowed, shook some hands and kissed others, and sat down with the lovely women. It was Lord Rutland. Short, slim, elegant to the point of affectation, he had more natural wit than education. A good conversationalist, rather skeptical and mocking, he was a trifle arrogant but avoided insolence. The proud possessor of a long line of ances-

---

henaten's son Tutankhamun was originally named Tutank-haten, but Amun's name was substituted for Aten's, reflecting the reversion to older rites that Ormus draws upon in his ficti-tious account of Tutankhamun's life.

tors, he glorified himself in numbering among them the illustrious supposed author of the works of William Shakespeare, and when his intellect was clouded by slight intoxication he would start reminiscing about the works of his ancestor Roger Manners, Earl of Rutland, born at Belvoir Castle in Leicestershire in 1576.[8]

The Duchess's vanity had latched on to that idea and she had sponsored research by an erudite bibliomaniac on the origin of the famous dramatist's works. He had battled with many contradictory texts, after which he had given birth to an enormous volume concluding that William Shakespeare of Stratford-on-Avon, who had held gentlemen's horses at theater doors in his youth, was merely a man of straw, paid and maintained to mask Roger Manners, Lord Rutland, a gentleman of the court, whose satirical portraits of the great might have won him many enemies, especially the disfavor of Queen Elizabeth.

The present Duke, whom literary polemics and that legend decorated with a certain distinction, had met a fifth-year student at the Harvard University named William Shakespeare; in order to give the legend even more vigor and further emphasis, it had amused him to befriend that Bohemian, who corresponded well enough to the character of one of Shakespeare's heroes, Sir John Falstaff. Since then, William had gone everywhere with Lord Rutland, lived largely at his expense, without a

---

[8] Roger Manners, the fifth Earl of Rutland (after the recreation of the title) married the daughter of Sir Philip Sidney, the author of *Arcadia*. He was suggested as a possible author of Shakespeare's plays by Karl Bleibtreu in *Der Wahre Shakespeare* (1907), but the briefly fashionable theory soon fell out of favor.

care in the world and with complete freedom of speech. People even made jokes behind their backs about their uncertain amity. Diana liked the buffoon well enough, and helped him to personify her husband's illustrious ancestry. Furthermore, the Duke, in his aristocratic pride, shared his wife's ideas regarding survival after death. Can one, when one is a Duke, disappear like some obscure manual laborer or animal? In other matters, George Manners, Duke of Rutland was a philosopher and a mocker, but without overmuch acidity.

"Astonishing, astonishing, what you just said, my dear Lady Love! I think there's a lot of charlatanry in it, but this Mage Ormus must be amusing to listen to. We must have him. He'll give us a rest from all this spiritualist nonsense, which has given us a veritable indigestion."

"At the Duchess's instigation," said the Margrave von Weringen, "I've read all the occult authors: Allan Kardec, Colonel Rochas, Stanislas de Guaita, Léon Denis, Thomas Lake Harris, Madame Blavatsky, D. D. Home, Henry Slade and others, but I'm confused by all their theories, which are totally lacking in detail. At least Mage Ormus has the advantage of being precise—and then again, one can see him."

"One might perhaps even be able to touch him," sniggered the Duke. "Women need prophets who are palpable, who need to eat, drink and..."

"Duke, Duke!" said Mary O'Brien, scandalized.

"Forgive me, Miss Ireland! I forgot that your democratic feminism is coupled with a rather old-fashioned severity."

"Why are you always teasing poor Mary?" said the Duchess.

"Let's not get off the subject," said Kate Souvermann. "Mage Ormus has promised to come to my soirée tomorrow. Would you all like to come?"

"Are men admitted?" asked the Duke.

"Certainly. Bring your husbands and admirers. After the sorcerer, there'll be dancing."

"Bravo! There'll be resistance to suggestion, then."

"On which note I'll leave you," Kate said. "I have preparations to make."

"Can I bring Shakespeare?" asked the Duke.

"Yes—what would you do without your Double? You'd be like a body without a soul."

II. The Incantation

The banker Souvermann's town house was also on Fifth Avenue. It was a house in the Cubist style: uncomfortable furniture, but modern. In Karl Souvermann's house everything was modern: the decoration, the paintings, everything. A vast library, also very modern, contained modern books, large folios in richly decorated morocco bindings: books that one does not read, the pages uncut, by famous and tedious authors whom no one reads but are much admired. Souvermann was very proud of his library. He had manuscripts by Valéry, Proust and Cucu.[9] In that vast room he had gathered his privileged friends for the reception of the Mage Ormus. The latter had said that he would arrive at ten o'clock; people were expectant.

The Duke and Duchess of Rutland had arrived first, accompanied by Mary O'Brien and the inseparable William Shakespeare. Marc Pytor, the journalist, was surrounded. He read out a dispatch from Alexandria, and the elite gathered at the Souvermann residence, lovers of the more-or-less occult sciences, were very interested in the research of the British mission.

"It's exciting," said Diana.

"Do you know," said Marc Pytor, "that the Egyptians don't look kindly on these excavations? They say that the Pharaohs will avenge themselves for having been reawakened before time, for mummies need to wait five thousand years before quitting their Double to

---

[9] The third name might be misrendered, but is more probably a joke. The English equivalent of the name would be Cuckoo.

reenter the bosom of Osiris. If so, I one wouldn't want to be in the skin of Lord Carnarvon's successors."

"Me neither," said Shakespeare. "The robbers of the Pharaohs' tombs all paid with their lives for that sacrilege. Why shouldn't the imitators of the late Carnarvon suffer the same fate as their predecessors? Lords and fellahs are equal before death. It only requires the bite of a fly."

"Let's not disturb mysterious Egypt," said the engineer Pall Herald, "and leave these troubling adventures to the unemployed of the Old World."

"We have equally interesting research to carry out here. The cradle of the two Americas has scarcely been glimpsed. Peruvian relics also indicate a very ancient civilization on our own continent."

"If the Bible mentioned it, perhaps we might concern ourselves with it—but Jehovah completely forgot about the New World. In his time, obviously, America hadn't been discovered."

"You're impious, Mr. Shakespeare!" exclaimed the Irishwoman.

Finally, a lackey announced: "Sir Antal Fodor." Antal Fodor was the secular name of the Mage Ormus.

At the sight of the newcomer, everyone had the impression of a dominator. The Mage Ormus was tall, and beneath his impeccable suit one divined an admirably-proportioned body. His face, its pallor ocher-tinted, was that of an Indian Bacchus, illuminated by splendid golden yellow eyes; his hair and eyebrows were blue-black, thick and smooth, framing an admirably monumental forehead. He came forward casually and bowed slightly. Instinctively, everyone got to their feet to return that gesture.

Kate Souvermann extended her hand to him, which he gallantly raised to his lips. Kate introduced him, this time saying: "The Mage Ormus."

"Do you know what we were talking about when you arrived?" she asked.

The thought-reader did not hesitate. "The honorable John Flatsbury was regretting that America is neglecting to dig into its ground, as the English are doing in that of ancient Egypt."

"You're a marvelous diviner," exclaimed Diana. "Can you explain that astonishing faculty to us?"

"Everyone can acquire it, Milady. It's a question of study—rather specialized, it's true, but which I'll try to enable you to understand. Until recent years, the people who have concerned themselves with physical and chemical sciences have only been concerned, so to speak, with palpable forces. However, we utilize fluidic forces that we produce without ever having analyzed them—electricity and magnetism, for example. Then another force was discovered, which combines the two, and has revealed to us the force and subdivision of waves. The electromagnetic waves utilized by people as a means of telegraphy and telephony are only a beginning. Our brains can also become receivers of waves vibrating around us. For someone initiated into that invisible language, nothing can remain unknown. By means of a kind of internal vibration, he can hear all the sounds and see all the images emitted around him, within a radius that has no limit other than his own willpower."

"But what is it necessary to do to acquire that knowledge and that gift?"

"Study—study incessantly. One obtains that goal by means of a kind of isolation of one's psychic 'self,' which is the component of our personality that does not die…any more, in fact, than our material fraction, which is also transformed. But that material part is only our 'self' during a lifetime, while the psychic part remains, for a certain number, their 'self' forever. A person who, by means of study, is sufficiently detached from matter to recover his 'memory,' can thus revive the past and see its different incarnations again."

"Brr!" whispered Shakespeare in the Duke's ear. "It's not very clear, but it gives one a terrible thirst. I regret not having a bottle in my pocket."

"But you're very young to have arrived at that psychic perfection."

"If I'd only had the time of my present life to study, it would be impossible—but the knowledge of my anterior existences augments it with the knowledge accumulated during those other lives."

"A few days ago, you recounted an episode of an anterior life at Countess Olivani-Sforza's house. Can you give us a few details about the Pharaoh whose tomb the English mission is researching?"

Antal Fodor smiled. "In one of my previous existences, I *was* the Pharaoh Tutankhamun."

"So psychic transmigration isn't a myth!" said the Duchess.

"I'm the living proof of it. It would be the same for you, if you had a less ephemeral memory. It's simply a faculty to consolidate. It requires a gift, and practice—the gift first."

"Easy to say, but not so easy to do. How?"

Shakespeare replied: "By drinking enough to see double, or triple. That happens to me sometimes—I lose my personality. It's only a matter of disentangling in myself the different persons confused in my brain. It's then that the numerous heroes of my namesake's plays mingle in my personality, and I'm Hamlet, Macbeth and Othello all at the same time. The Bacchic vapors give an appearance of reality to those illustrious illusions. Now that I have a conductive wire, thanks to the Mage Ormus, I'll only have to drink until I recover one of my personalities of past times."

"You'll certainly find yourself," said Lord Rutland, "in the skin of Sir John Falstaff."

"I repeat," Antal Fodor continued, without paying any heed to Shakespeare's digression, "that one acquires the faulty in question by the detachment and elevation of the mind over matter. There are individuals that your civilization considers as akin to madmen, the Yogis and Fakirs of India, who succeed in exteriorizing themselves to the point of reducing their material parts almost to nothing.

"I've seen a Yogi have himself buried at a depth of two meters; barley was sown on the place—and three weeks later, when the barley had begun to sprout, he was disinterred and came back to life. Others remain suspended by the feet for days on end and, having regained their feet, pick up the money that passers-by have thrown under the tree, and then repeat the same prodigy. These men have no scientific education; they're unaware of our applications of electricity and magnetism—but those ignorant men, more expert than we are in matters of fluidic force, know how to make use of them from the viewpoint of autosuggestion, and obtain amazing phenomena therefrom.

"It's by studying with brahmins and fakirs that I've learned the little that I know, but it required my preceding incarnations. The main thing is to obtain the perpetuity of the memory, and not all our existences are worth the trouble of recalling. Only a few thousand men and women have an intellectual life worthy of being used in another individuality, and only a few hundred have a heredity worthy of being followed through the centuries

"Great intelligences are rare, and the men of genius of our century are the sum of defunct geniuses; the fluidic immortality of the mind is not for everyone. It's necessary to have a terrestrial soul like a marvelous diamond among negligible pebbles."

"You told us that you were the Pharaoh Tutankhamun. Would you be kind enough to tell us about him...I beg your pardon, about *yourself*, in that epoch?"

"Gladly," said the Mage.

He began immediately, in a voice that was assured, but as if internal. He seemed to be groping in the darkness of centuries in order to find the light. Then his voice was gradually raised, and soon resumed its normal timbre.

"I can see myself after the death of my father, Pharaoh Shaakera-Amun.[10] I was fourteen then. I had been married two years before to the daughter of the high priest of Amon, That-ni-Hilla. At dawn, Aphi-Omra invited me to go down into the subterranean parts of the temple of Amon-Ra, to witness the initial preparations for the embalming of the deceased Pharaoh. In accord-

---

[10] It had not been confirmed in 1929 that Akhenaten was Tutanhkamun's father, but the two pharaohs who reigned briefly in between the two were Semkhkare and Nerferneferu-aten, so this name appears to have been improvised, like the others cited. Tutankhamun's actual consort was Ankhsena-mun.

ance with the custom, I would only be the sacred Pharaoh—which is to say, emperor and god—when Shaakera was at rest in his hypogeum, where I, his successor, had to preside over his funeral rites.

"Embalming takes two moons, and that time would be employed in my education as a Pharaoh. Until then, I had lived like all the nobles of the Empire; now my royal and divine life was about to begin.

"Aphi-Omra initiates me, cuts me and severs my facial muscles, in order that my face will remain as motionless as a bronze mask; my mouth will no longer be able to smile, or my eyelids to descend. It is necessary that my human face become a divine mask.

"The people do not know me. I have never appeared in public, for no one must know that I have been a child, that I have passed through all the phases of adolescence. The son of a god must have nothing in common with humankind. Until my marriage, I never emerged from the gynaeceum, and marriage was required as soon as I reached the age of puberty, for it is necessary that there should be an heir to the throne as soon as possible. Aphi-Omra is ambitious; he wants to reign over me as he reigned over my father.

"The day when I descended into the embalming room was a revelation, thanks to the cerebral tension I experienced before the Pharaoh's cadaver. Until then, I had not seen any corpses except those of slaves that I had killed in anger or disappointment—but my father was a Pharaoh! It was a god that was in front of me, a horrible rag, emptied of entrails and brain, and the operators were getting ready to put him in a vat of salt for thirty days.

"Suddenly, then, I had a memory of another funeral ceremony; I saw another cadaver, and I was conscious that it had been me. Then that image was effaced—but it had made its impression. The child, the puppet, king and god who had to act in accordance with the hand of the high priest, no longer existed; there was a thought within me, a will. The new Pharaoh wanted to be something other than an effigy, and a struggle began between Aphi-Omra and his college.

"The contest was not easy. I was alone. Not one chief, not one soldier, could be useful to me, not knowing me. I could only count on one aide, That-ni-Hilla—but my wife was the high priest's daughter. What could I do? By chance, I overheard a conversation between Aphi-Omra and the Levite Yacoub, an Israelite he had converted. It was about an ancient cult whose vigor the priests of Heliopolis were renewing, with a few variations. For the priests of Amon, that was a danger; they feared that the new cult might spread through Egypt and reach Thebes. I understood that if I could enter into communication with the priests of Heliopolis, I would have allies there. But how? Finally, I had an idea...

"After completing the sacred rite among the dead, Aphi-Omra takes me home. The part of the gynaeceum reserved for me is a palace situated beside the sacred lake. I have never been to the city, but thanks to That-ni-Hilla I know the layout of the temples and palaces. To carry out my plan, I need to get out of the sacred enclosure. This is what I have to do: put a letter to the high priest of Heliopolis into a small wooden box, and confide my precious message to a boatman—or, if I can't find one, to the Nile. Osiris will protect me and guide the box to its destination.

"I wrote my letter and leave the palace furtively. Fortunately, the night is moonless. I slip alongside the temple of Aminothis, and get over the wall by climbing up the angle of a colonnade. In front of me, three or four hundred paces away, is the temple of the divine Korsou, then that of the goddess Apelt, and finally the avenue of the sphinxes, by which I can reach the Nile.[11]

"My hopes are thwarted; the temple of Apelt blocks my way; the gateway set at the extremity of the avenue of the sphinxes is closed by a bronze door, and on my right is the wall of the enclosure, manned by armed sentinels. So I, the king and god, am a prisoner in my own city, my own palace; it's necessary for me to turn round and go back, still hiding, for the patrols are circulating. A terrible anger rises within me against those priests who are in possession of absolute power. Oh, how I hate that Aphi-Omra, and also That-ni-Hilla, his daughter and my wife!

"I understand now all the desire and ambition of those people. I've been married for two years, and my wife is still sterile. The priest doesn't want me to have a heir, and with me dead, the throne will belong to That-ni-Hilla—to his daughter, who shares her father's ideas and cupidity. The small details of my conjugal life surge forth in my thoughts, confirming my suspicions..."

In the course of this long story, related in a voice whose inflections were cleverly calculated to act on the nerves of the women who were attached, above all, to the physical plane, the narrator had succeeded in creating a collective illusion.

The Mage Ormus disappeared, to give way to the Pharaoh, of whom he was seen to have taken on the face.

---

[11] All three of the names attached to these temples appear to be improvised, although "Aminothis" might coonceivably be a misrendering of "Amenophis."

The ambience had now become filled with mysterious fluids and invisible presences, and everyone felt transported to an epoch whose evocation appeared to be a ludicrous anachronism in that ultra-modern décor.

"But who's that? A white form has emerged from the temple of Korsou; it quits the shadows of the high columns and comes toward me. The night is bright now. The fog that rises from the Nile at nightfall has dissipated. The sky is swarming with stars. The woman is carrying a basket, which seems to be very heavy.

"Hidden behind a pillar, I watch. Ten paces away from me, she stops, puts down her burden and rests for a moment. How beautiful she is! I've forgotten the objective of my escapade. Dazzled by admiration, I advance toward her. She utters a cry of fright, tries to flee—but I already have her in my arms.

"'The Pharaoh!' she cries.

"'You know me?'

"'I've seen you from the terraces of the temple, strolling around the sacred lake,'

"'Where are you going with that basket?'

"'To take kitchen debris to the sacred crocodiles.'

"'What's your name?'

"'Am-Phaoli.'

"'I love you, Am-Phaoli.'

"'O Pharaoh, I am your servant.'

"And, abandoning everything, I draw her into the shadow of the temple. When we come back, Am-Phaoli picks up her basket.

"'It's heavy,' I say. 'I want to help you.'

"She laughs. 'Oh! Pharaoh!'

"A thought occurs to me. 'Can you go out into the city?'

"'Once a month. I'm not a slave but a hireling. My family lives in Pheliap and works among the hypogea.'

"'Can you get this box to Heliopolis?'

"'Nothing simpler. My brother Hit-Mouth is a boatman on the Nile and can take it.'

"'And when are you going out?'

"'In seven days.'

"'That's good—but I want to see you again. Do you carry out this task every night?'

"'Only every second night. Tomorrow it will be Respah.'

"'Well then, I'll wait for you the day after tomorrow.'

"I pick up the basket and I go to empty it into the sacred lake. Then Am-Phaoli goes away, taking the box with her…and my heart...

"For the first time, I'm in love..."

Momentarily, Ormus' handsome face was illuminated by a flame of love, which transfigured it. His eyes, drowned by ecstasy, brushed all he female gazes extended toward him like a kiss, lingering slightly on the Duchess. Then he resumed.

"Days have followed one another; I'm a king and god; truly, by virtue of love and power, I'm the Master. The military chiefs obey me; I have devoted and faithful friends. I've had Aphi-Omra assassinated and I've repudiated That-ni-Hilla, in order to raise Am-Phaoli, whom I love and who loves me, to my level. I'm a father; I can actively occupy myself with my Double. My wife's relatives have general responsibility for the Theban hypogea. I shall have a well-constructed and well-hidden sepulcher...

"Days follow one another. I'm feared; the priests and Amon tremble before me. I'm thinking of reestablishing the old cult of the Sun, of Osiris, but it's necessary for me to reformulate my genealogy; my theologians are busy with that. I'm twenty-six years old. In spite of my precautions, the priests of Amon succeed in poisoning me, but I'm dying in peace even so. Am-Phaoli has three daughters; the eldest is seven; she's energetic and clever; she'll be able to defend her rank and mine..."

The Mage Ormus stopped. Everyone in the library was hanging on to his lips. His eyes scanned the audience members in turn, bathing them, so to speak, with their magnetic effluvia, imposing absolute belief upon them.

The Duchess of Rutland felt that it was to her, most of all, that the strange theosophist was speaking, his gaze hammering her mind, already disposed to mysticism, with its suggestive power. At the evocation of ancient life, it seemed to her that she had lived in that era. She had thought at first that she was the daughter of the high priest Aphi-Omra; then, when Am-Phaoli appeared, she had sensed, and the eyes of the Mage Ormus had told her, speaking to her once again, that this time, it really was her.

So, she had been a Pharaoh's wife—and her submissive eyes had fixed themselves on the Mage, on the Pharaoh.

And everyone else, regardless of what they believed, was impressed by that evocation of ancient Egyptian life. Kate Souvermann was triumphant. It was in her house that such a success had been won.

She took possession of Ormus. "Oh, Master, what a marvelous story! So you have lived that glorious life of an ancient monarch! Oh, how I wish that I had the same gift of retrospective memory!"

"Master," asked the Duchess of Rutland, "would you consent to teach me?"

Ormus bowed. "It would be quite rapid, for we have already encountered one another in the past. But you heard what I said: it requires study and determination." And the Mage, subjugating her with his gaze, extended an imperious hand toward her.

All the women surrounded Ormus, soliciting the favor of a similar soirée.

The Mage spoke again. "Ladies and gentlemen," he said, "my life is devoted to my work. In Europe I have founded a religion in rapport with the modern mind: a scientific, moral and sane religion, the only logical religion, based on respect for and veneration of out All-Father, the divine Sun: Helios, Osiris. It's nothing but an old myth that I'm rejuvenating, you see. Respect and veneration, I said, without prayer, which is an insult to the divinity. Perhaps I shall offend a few ideas in that, but reflect. Prayer is not a humility but a vanity. It assumes that the person making use of it, lost among millions of others, will have the power to attract the attention of the divinity to one of his creatures. The real god, the regulator of worlds, has no preferences, and a blade of grass, a centenarian oak, and insect and Poincaré[12] are all equal before him."

He paused momentarily, and then went on: "The sect that I have founded is called the Flower of Truth. In

---

[12] It is not obvious whether this reference is to the mathematician Henri Poincaré or the statesman Raymond Poincaré, but Champsaur's readers would have been far more familiar with the latter.

order for that flower to blossom and produce offspring, in order that it might extend and cover the globe, I need the collaboration of all people of good will. Already, in Europe, writers, artists and scientists—all thinking people—are rallying to my banner. A prophet of that religion of light and progress, I travel the world to sow the good seed. I hope that in New York, the center of light and progress, I shall find both a good welcome and solid collaboration."

"What you need, above all, is an organ of propaganda," said Marc Pytor. "I'll put my paper, the *Daily Mail*, at your disposal."

"And I," said the Duchess of Rutland, "am thinking of founding an illustrated magazine with you: *Old Life*. It won't be bad business; since the Great War, mystical ideas are revealing dancing in popularity."

"I welcome all collaboration, all useful support."

"Money," muttered Shakespeare. "I'm dying of thirst, old chap." He took Rutland's arm. "Let's get out of here, George."

III. The Chamber of Stars

There was a single-story detached house at the extremity of a peaceful suburb, not yet invaded by the hectic life of commerce and finance. The small building affected the form of a Greek temple, with a façade of slender columns supporting an attic on which a sculptor who was far from being a Phidias had grouped gods and goddesses. Antal Fodor had rented it and appropriated its interior to its new purpose. It is necessary that a fakir's chapel should have an appearance capable of influencing the imagination of the credulous.

Only the consultation room, or conference room, had an appropriate decoration. It was the largest room in the house. It could hold fifty people, at a stretch. The floor was covered was dark blue, almost black carpet, and the walls were hung with fabric in the same hue, with the principal constellations designed thereon with silvery stars. The whole created an impression of sidereal immensity. Stuck to the star-strewn ceiling, a large dark blue shallow basin of frosted glass provided the only light, the room having no apparent door or windows.

An old man dressed in an ample white robe was crouched in the oriental manner beneath that luminous opaline medusa, and was plunged in reflection, with his forehead supported by his hand.

One o'clock sounded in the next room.

"He's late," he murmured,

As if by way of reply, a sheet of fabric was lifted up and Antal Fodor came into the room—and the gentleman in the suit and top hat made a disconcerting contrast with

41

the man in the white robe, in that celestial décor—a contrast as disconcerting as the one that must exist between their two mentalities.

"They kept you a long time," moaned the old man, getting up. He was tall and his face seemed to be majestically crowned by thick white hair; a long beard in a style reminiscent of Michelangelo, flowing over his white robe, gave him a Biblical aspect, or that of Father Mope,[13] one of the last disciples of the Swedish thaumaturge Emmanuel Swedenborg, the celebrated illuminator who had astonished the eighteenth century with his revelations.

Adsum, born in Norway, was a lumber-room of human knowledge; he added to his model's mystical aspect all modern scientific knowledge and all philosophical hypotheses. Having met Antal Fodor in India, he had realized how useful the young man, as handsome as a god, might be to him. He had made him part of a new religion, intelligent and commercial, and had entered into an alliance with him.

Adsum was one of those illuminati who, having created an idea, devoted himself to it passionately. Fodor's own faith was mediocre; he saw it above all as a means to wealth and domination. In sum, the two individuals complemented one another. Both were possessed of a curious intellectual force.

"Well?"

"It went marvelously. I have them all." He set his shiny hat down on a cushion, lit a cigarette and told the old savant all about the soirée and its result: the assured

---

[13] As this name is presumably intended to evoke an image in the reader's mind it seems unlikely that it is improvised, but if it is not, it must be misrendered.

support of Pytor and Melcom, influence over the Duchess of Rutland, and so on.

"Good," said Adsum. "Our doctrine addresses an elite. After the gods of Olympus, who had nothing beneath their myths, in sum, but the adoration of nature, and after the supremacy of Christianity over the poor in spirit, it's finally time for the reign of reason. Our hope lies in America, the issue of Old Europe. Such a race, without the old atavism of idolatry, ought to have already created a philosophy capable of reducing all religious fanaticism to annihilation."

"What are you saying, Master? It seems to me that you're overshooting the target. Humans are, above all, lovers of the marvelous. If we have some success, it's because of our magical science. It's necessary that they retain somewhat in awe of us, as superhumans. As in all religions, it's necessary to make the most of it."

"It's necessary to reign over minds, my Son, not over strong-boxes. Let's focus on one ideal—and as a means of propaganda, we only need one thing: Diana Bering's colossal fortune. It's necessary, in everyone's eyes to be disinterested. Do you think that those who come to us won't weigh our actions and our words? All religions have addressed themselves, above all, to the humble and the innocent. We'll do the opposite, in order that the concentration of intelligence will bring us close to the knowledge of the great mystery. Ormus, you haven't yet completely got rid of your old self. All you see in my dream is a means of becoming rich and powerful—but I, your Master, only see a means of centralizing intelligence in order to discover the truth. Material assistance is, however, indispensable to us. The Duchess, then…?"

"In my hands, she will be the instrument that you've judiciously chosen. At the age when bored women are attracted to the occult sciences, her vanity will be flattered by the role played by her in an anterior life. I've suggested an entire filiation: the wife of a Pharaoh. Cleopatra, the Empress Eudoxia, what do I care? Her brain's already working and building on it." Taking a puff on his cigarette, he concluded: "The woman's mine, I tell you."

"Not yet, for you're not sure of yourself."

"Yes, two mentalities are competing within me. The words escaping my lips create dupes, and I feel myself that I'm an impostor. During my tale of the life of Tut-Ankh-Amun, my mind, extended toward that objective, suggested to the Duchess of Rutland that she had been the Pharaoh's wife: Am-Phaoli, the loving wife of the Egyptian king and god. She has no inkling of the upstart Antal Fodor; for her, I'm the Mage Ormus, the last incarnation of vanished superior beings. But if others believe in me, O Master, I still doubt."

Adsum took a step forward. Majestic in his ample white robe, he placed a hand on the other's shoulder, and, staring into his eyes with steel-gray eyes that did not blink, he said: "It's necessary to have no doubt, my son. Doubt weakens the will, and you don't have the right to that, my pupil, my spiritual child. Look into the past. You have been the Pharaoh Tut-Ankh-Amun, just as I have been the great pontiff of Heliopolis, the regenerator of the ancient and only true religion: worship of the Sun.

Antal Fodor bowed, and Adsum placed his thumb at the root of the nose. Looking him straight in the eyes, the latter said: "In the name of the Father, in the name of the Sun, escape your wretched form and remount the ladder of elapsed centuries. Let your mind, liberated from all bonds, traverse seas and deserts, and follow my thought. The Father, who is in the sky, has just surged over the horizon. Above the desert plains of Arabia, his rays illuminate the obelisks and the tall pylons of the temples of Thebes. Look! At the far end of the narrow and long row of gigantic columns, on a throne of gold and precious stones, a young man in the hieratic stance of the great granite gods is motionless, seemingly seeing nothing of trivial human life. Is he a man? Is he a god? Both. He is as young and beautiful as spring, that master of old Egypt. Do you recognize him?"

"Yes, it's me."

"Then why do you speak of doubt?"

"Because I'm still too attached to matter. I have to deceive the Duchess, then? Suggest a lie to her?"

"Perhaps it isn't one. I know nothing about Lady Rutland except what you've told me. Do you have news from Europe?"

"Yes, Master. The Flower of Truth is growing, slowly but surely. We need propaganda though—we need, if necessary, to maintain those who come to us. For that we need money, which is the master prior to the mind."

"This billionairess must be ours! And to be ours, she needs to have faith. She will believe, because we'll teach her the truth. Don't hesitate any longer to speak with the faith that moves mountains. At your voice, the dead will rise up from their graves to aid us."

IV. A Savant Flirt

Built on a hundred-meter hill, Redge House overlooked the surroundings of Long Island, and from its windows, one could see the green waters of the Atlantic crawling. The façade was in the somewhat staid but harmonious style of the French architect Gabriel. As for the grounds, they were large and eccentric. It was there that Diana felt most tranquil, and received her habitual companions in the magical art—and it was there that she had asked the Mage Ormus to come to instruct her.

And for a month already, he had been initiating the Duchess in the great mysteries. While admiring and sharing the theologian's doctrines, she could not separate the man from the savant, and without being aware of it she was subject to masculine influence, aspiring to new sensations—and the Mage sensed that he had only to say the word to change the pupil into a mistress. He knew, however, that the lover would compromise the sorcerer, and he carefully avoided the instruction going down that road. The Duchess, moreover, had already donated a million to their common ideal: the Flower of Truth. The handsome adventurer's ambition was aiming much higher.

"So," said the Duchess, "I was your future queen, Am-Phaoli, who took food to the sacred crocodiles? And in a subsequent incarnation, the divine Cleopatra?"

"And I the triumvir Mark Antony. Do you remember?"

"Yes, when you're here."

"That's because you haven't yet succeeded in isolating your mind. The exteriorization isn't complete. It's necessary to focus your will, disengage yourself from its material envelope."

"I'm trying to do that, but I need to be helped."

The Mage, suddenly straightening up, put his hands on his breast and closed his eyes. He seemed to be concentrating all his will-power internally. Abruptly, the splendid golden eyes darted their gaze at the Duchess, who shuddered as if she had received an electric shock.

Then the Mage spoke.

"The sun is rising over Alexandria. I've spent the night with Cleopatra, the immortal charmer. Accompanied by the physician Philotas, I'm going to the harbor to talk to Sextus Aphissa, the great captain of the Egyptian fleet. Caesar has declared war on Egypt, under the pretext that I've exceeded my authority in proclaiming Cleopatra an independent queen, with her son Caesarion as a successor.

"The Egyptian fleet, more than a hundred galleys strong, could easily stand up to Caesar if it were well-equipped with oarsmen. Unfortunately, there's a shortage of mariners, and ships too. Sextus Aphissa has been trying hard to recruit oarsmen from the islands, and that's why I'm going to the harbor. I'm chatting with Philotas when a trireme comes in to dock at a junction of the quay. 'Mark Antony!' shouts a voice.

"I turn round; sitting in the stern, a woman wearing the costume of a palace servant beckons to me. I go forward; then I hear a loud burst of laughter and I recognize Cleopatra in disguise. 'Climb aboard!' she says to me. I jump on to the vessel, followed by Philotas.

"'Forgive me,' says the queen. 'I thought that you wanted to deceive me, and I came to make sure that your meeting with Sextus was real. Come on, Sextus is aboard.'

"Indeed, Aphissa shows himself. 'Greetings, Augustus! I only have sixty galleys, but I know, from a reliable source, that the Romans only have thirty-two, each with only a single rank of oarsmen.'

"Philotas intervenes. 'Caesar's mariners are battle-hardened, and I have no confidence in your heavy galleys with three ranks; you'd do better to take your chances with the land army.'

"That's also my opinion, but the queen wants to see a naval battle. 'I want my trireme to be in the first rank,' she commands, 'and Caesar will see whether I'm worthy to rule Egypt.'

"'Isn't it enough to reign over Antony's heart?' asks Philotas.

"'Since Antony has betrayed me to marry Octavia, I doubt his constancy.'

"'Would I be here if I had wanted to please Caesar's sister? Mark Antony is entirely yours.'

"'Then let Antonia obey me. In the meantime, Sextus, I desire to take an excursion by sea and go to eat oysters at Marhissa.'

"'That would be extremely imprudent, O Queen, and for Caesar, there would be no capture as fine as that of our two sovereigns by the enemy fleet in that little fishing village.'

"The queen stamps her foot. 'Let's go, or I'll believe that you're afraid.'

"Sextus Aphissa turns the ship about in order to obey the queen's caprice. Now we're following the coast in the direction of Marhissa.

"We've been sailing for an hour when we find ourselves confronting three Roman triremes. Sextus immediately leaps down to the oar-deck, and we come about so close to the enemy that the leading ship brushes our stern. 'Faster! Faster! Freedom for all if we escape!' Our vessel flies over the waves—but the Roman galleys are gaining on us. While one of them gives chase, the other two make haste to cut us off.

"'We're doomed,' says Philotas. 'The lighter Roman galleys will surround us.' The situation is critical. Fortunately, the Romans fear a trap. The point of Bura-Agieh, which we're approaching, might conceal an ambush. That's why the other two ships have gone on ahead in order to explore the shore. The coast is no more than a hundred fathoms away. I launch myself on to the false deck, where Sextus is spurring on the oarsmen, and I tell him my plan.

"He approves, and I go back up. The two Roman triremes, having ascertained that there's no one behind the cape, are pursuing up at top speed. Suddenly, on an order from Sextus, our rowers stop, and then begin rowing backwards.

"The Romans, who didn't expect that maneuver, come at us at top speed and crash into our vessel, which is heavier than theirs. They take on water immediately, and sink. We head straight for the coast and launch out skiff on to the sand.

"I pick Cleopatra up in my arms and jump into the water. The oarsmen and one of the chiefs do the same, and now we're all running toward the city. A volley of arrows falls behind us, wounding the unfortunate Philotas grievously.

"An hour later, we get back to Alexandria, and you say, once you've recovered from your emotion: 'Hurry up, Antony, and beat the Romans, so that I can go and eat oysters at Marhissa.'"

"Do you remember that excursion at sea?"

"I remember having a little fright on that beautiful day, my dear Mage, but I don't remember the night before."

Ormus did not appear to understand the allusion. He continued: "That wasn't the first time that you'd tried Antony's patience and courage. You were as whimsical as you were beautiful, and the triumvir was subjected to rude proofs by your whims."

"Mark Antony, what do you think of Cleopatra?"

"Enchantress, no man could resist your charms."

"And I love you too—until death!"

"Don't lie to the past," said the Mage. "If Cleopatra hadn't feared being attached to Caesar's chariot as a captive, you wouldn't have killed yourself. Our mutual majesty permitted us to deliver ourselves shamelessly and unstintingly to any excess; we used and abused it. It was an epoch when everything was done on a lavish scale. For me, that incarnation had no spiritual profit—on the contrary; it was a complete triumph of materialism, almost a moral regression."

"And for me? For Cleopatra, I mean?"

"You never had any objective other than sensual satisfaction, and did not think much. You're making progress, as you can see."

"Yes, perhaps—but I don't regret having been Cleopatra."

V. The Eternal Triangle

At that moment, an automobile horn resounded in the avenue leading to Redge House. The Duchess darted a glance outside.

"My husband!" she said, I a tone of annoyance. "I thought he was with the Olivani-Sforzas. He's bringing his inseparable Will here."

"That drunken buffoon, always mocking. How can the Duke compromise himself in the company of such a clown?"

"For us, Shakespeare is a parasite. He's by no means stupid, and his company has often helped me to tolerate that of the Duke—but since I've come to know you, they seem as annoying as one another. They've come to disturb my initiation again."

"I've noticed," said Ormus, "that the Duke, who welcomed me benevolently at first, seems less well-disposed toward me now."

"He's somewhat subject to the influence of Shakespeare, a thoroughgoing materialist, and as soon as my husband escapes your influence, he falls back under his friend's unfortunate sway."

"I'll go, then. When do you want to continue your studies, Madame?"

"This coming and going between here and New York is intolerable. I'm going to speak to George about putting you up at Redge House. That way, I'll have you more to myself. The season's about to start; all of fashionable society will be here on Long Island before long. It's in your interest—the interests of our work—for us to be together."

Having had himself announced, the Duke came into the drawing room. "Ah!" he said. "You're in conference with your Mage! Hello, my dear chap." He kissed the Duchess's hand. "Is you pupil making progress?"

"I've just offered the Mage Ormus hospitality at Redge House," Diana interjected, "which would thus become the active center of our doctrine, the Flower of Truth. Would you please make the arrangements for the Master's accommodation?"

"Certainly…certainly…"

"I'll leave you, then," said Diana, standing up.

"Follow me," said Lord Rutland to the Mage, after the Duchess's departure. "I need to talk to you, and I don't like talking without a drink."

VI. The Forbidden Bar

Reformist laws do not apply to billionaires, and prohibition imposed on sin only makes it more attractive; a glass of alcohol drunk in secret has a completely different flavor from those quaffed in times when one could drink without impediment. The dry regime was prevalent throughout the United States, and yet the number of measures taken against drunkards was increasing incessantly. Drinkers fell back on clubs, where clandestine barmen poured the forbidden liquids discreetly.

In imitation of the clubs, rich houses competed in luxury and comfort in the installation of secret bars. George Manners, gladly conforming with this fashion, had therefore installed a bar in his apartment, skillfully disposed so as to be invisible to profane eyes. All the mystery, however, was more to satisfy convention than by virtue of veritable utility, for he had no reason to fear the slightest risk of a search—but it is fun to mock laws, especially when they are futile.

The bar at Redge House was a veritable marvel. Large panels of Japanese silk representing birds and flowers alternated with lacquered woodwork encrusted with nacre and gold. Behind the bar of waxed oak, a large leather panel of embossed leather represented the triumph of Bacchus. There were high chairs of curved wood, divans upholstered in Cordovan leather as broad and deep as beds, and Oriental carpets thick enough to deaden potential falls. Service was insured by an accomplished barman, who disappeared only to reappear at the summons of an electric button. The room was ventilated by an invisible shaft to the outside, running behind a thick ledge of sculpted and gilded wood surrounding the discreet room, admirably disposed for sacrifices to the god Alcohol. One entered by means of the displacement of one of the Japanese panels, sliding along grooves.

It was into this secluded bar that the Duke introduced Antal Fodor. William Shakespeare, installed on a stool at the high counter, was discussing a cocktail of his composition with the barman.

"Take careful note. Master Guidevor: one third old Xeres, one third French cognac, as old as possible, a pinch of Cayenne, two cloves, a mussel, three crayfish and a duck's egg. Beat forcefully, freeze and finish off with dry Mumm. Tell me what you think. Aha! Here's our sorcerer. Honor to the Pharaoh Tut-Ankh-Amun! The possible descendant of William Shakespeare salutes you!"

The Duke of Rutland said: "One can't talk properly on these perches. Let's sit down at a table."

They sat down in profound armchairs, and William stretched out on a divan. When the barman had served three cocktails, he withdrew.

The Duke took a mouthful, coughed, scratched the tip of his nose, and said: "My dear Ormus, what I have to say to you is rather delicate, especially after what the Duchess has just decided. You interest me enormously, that's indisputable. You're plan for a new religion isn't banal, and it doesn't displease me to play the role of a founder member. But...well...hmmm...help me out, Will!"

"Illustrious Pharaoh," said Shakespeare, "you're not unaware that intelligence and ineptitude are contagious and can be caught, like diseases. In consequence, it's necessary to be careful of the company one keeps. My excellent friend, doubtless for that reason, is afraid of your contact; he's afraid of contagion."

"Explain yourself clearly, Duke," said Ormus. "I'll answer you in the same way."

The Duke bit the bullet. "I can't see without a certain dread the influence that you've obtained over the Duchess of Rutland. Before your arrival in New York she already had an excessive taste for the fantastic, occultism, spiritualism and all those more-or-less charlatanesque practices. Between ourselves, all that phantasmagoria, in which you excel, proves that you have astonishing erudition, and I must admit that I've taken a great interest in it myself, after the fashion of someone at a performance or a lecture—but this psychic prestidigitation has gone on long enough. In wanting to install all your apparatus of sorcery here, the Duchess has overstepped the mark. Your presence has become, for me tranquility, I won't say a danger, but a reason for anxiety. How much do you want to continue your propaganda elsewhere? A million? What do you say, eh? Is that enough?"

"No," said the Mage, coldly. "I'm worth more than that. Returning frankness for frankness, I'm not going. My life is here; I'm the true master of the situation here. In the course of past times, the Duchess has already belonged to me several times. These unions create a bond between us that I have no intention of breaking. Your wife feels the same. She must belong to me again; I shall be her husband again."

"That's a bit stiff! Damnable Mage! What about me?"

"The Duchess can divorce you if she wishes. Personally, I'm a partisan of free union, and I have no fear of a change of ideas. What does it matter to you? Diana

Bering bought your name. If she keeps it, she'll pay you for the rent. If she divorces you, she'll give you a pension sufficient for you to live well, and as you please."

"As you like it!" added Shakespeare.

"Enough joking! You're an adventurer of considerable scope and astonishing allure, I agree—but the farce is over, and I'll go to the law if I must."

The Mage smiled disdainfully. "Poor fellow! You can do whatever I wish." His gaze imposed a superior will on his victim. "You dare to defy me—me, who can make you a being devoid of personality! Me, who can, for example, suggest to you the idea of suicide! Me, who can knead you like soft wax! Dare, then—dare!"

Rutland struggled momentarily under the dominating gaze of the Mage Ormus.

William watched the scene with amazed bewilderment. "My God!" he muttered. "There's a specimen that's out of the ordinary! Come on, old chap; dig your heels in. Have a drink—that'll do the trick."

Antal Fodor's gaze quit the Duke and fixed upon the fat parasite.

"All right! All right!" grunted the obese individual, letting himself fall back on to the divan. "After all, the quarrel doesn't concern me. Settle it however you want."

Ormus picked up his glass and took a long sip. "Do you understand?" he said. "A large pension for you and a free hand for me."

The Duke shook himself. "You're too strong for me—it'll depend on the Duchess. A large pension and liberty? After all, I'm beginning to get tired of American democracy. What do you say, Will?"

"Nature forms strange fellows when the mood takes her, and Sir is one of them. Let's leave it. I accept the world for what it is: a theater where everyone has to play his role. Ours, for the moment, is passive—but with lots of cash, that's okay!"

"Let the Duchess do as she wishes, then," Ormus concluded. "She'll tell you herself what course to follow."

After a discreet knock, the lacquered door, over which the branches and flowers of a Japanese cherry-tree flowed, slid aside and disappeared. Diana came into the bar with the stride of Semiramis.

"So, gentlemen, I've driven you to this. What are you doing with my Mage?"

She rang, and ordered a syrup. The Mage, sensing that the situation was tense and resolved to burn his boat, turned to her.

"Madame," she said. "We were talking about you…and me. Annoyed by my daily presence, the Duke of Rutland has offered me a million to leave the United States."

Diana frowned, and favored her husband with an Olympian stare. "Really? And with what money would George Manners, Duke of Rutland, pay for that expulsion? Not with his own, for he has none. What did you reply?"

"That I had rights anterior to his. That you have been mine three times in the course of the centuries. The first time was when I was the Pharaoh Tut-Ankh-Amun and I seated you on one of the most ancient thrones in the world. The second time was when I was the triumvir Mark Antony and you were the divine Cleopatra. The third time, in Byzantium, was when you were the dazzling Empress Eudoxia."

The Duchess, flattered, smiled at Antal Fodor and held out her hand to him. With an infinitely regal gesture, Ormus raised it to his lips.

The Duke, however, said sarcastically: "At any rate, my dear sir, "Nathan Bering's daughter is now the Duchess of Rutland. It would be a comedown to become the wife of an adventurer without a name or resources."

"I have more of them than you, as you can see."

"Evidently," said the Duchess, "the mage Ormus has titles anterior to yours, my dear. He has been a Pharaoh, a king and a god."

Rutland laughed sardonically. "In those times, people worshiped beasts: a sacred crocodile or a sacred bull, or simply the ox Apis."

"Whose horns you wear, my dear spouse; add them to the foreground of your coat-of-arms."

Shakespeare intervened in order to deflect the overly sharp banter. "Personally, I admire that succession of illustrious human lives. However, if there's an immanent justice, those great crowned criminals and historic courtesans would be more deserving of psychic regression and ought not to excite the least vanity."

Antal Fodor released the straw through which he was sipping his cocktail. "There is only intellectual supremacy when one has succeeded, and the beauty of an action, affirmed by its success, covers by the grandeur of the accomplishment any harm it might do to the vulgar."

"A singular morality!"

"Morality is for the herd. The men and women of the elite are above morality and virtue. What are virtues? What are vices? The former are screens behind which the latter live. Doubtless, behind human genius, there is always stupidity. The title of Duke counts for nothing in the universal life and my ancient rank of Pharaoh or triumvir is worth less than the brain of a Shakespeare—not this one—a Balzac or a Victor Hugo."

"Which doesn't alter the fact," said stout Will, "that privileges have the supreme advantage of allowing those who possess them to live well. Personally, I only claim for an ancestor William Shakespeare, of whose dramas and comedies, it appears, my friend Rutland was the author. If that hypothesis is correct, he did the work, and I got the glory."

"Reassure yourself," the Mage said, in a bantering tone. "It was not a Duke of Rutland that breathed his genius into Shakespeare. For want of imagination, certain literary men, incapable of creating, content themselves with research and slanders, in which they are duped by their own incapacity."

That was the last straw. Excited, in any case, by the cocktails, which he had frequently renewed, the Duke took umbrage.

"You're overstepping the mark, Mage Ormus. Go to the Devil! Antony or Pharaoh, but the conquistador Antal Fodor today, you want to cast me side conclusively. What! You're denying my ancestor, Roger Manners, Duke of Rutland, his work of genius! I'm finally in revolt. Am I quibbling about your ancient incarnations, or even your sorcerer's trickery and intrigue, which you're using for the conquest of a modern golden fleece? But I won't give up my place to you."

"That's enough!" the Duchess interjected. "I'll be the sole judge of that. The day when it pleases me to reclaim my liberty—which I never lost—I'll set the price, and, gentleman that you are, you'll accept my conditions."

These words had the effect on the Duke of a cold shower. He emptied his glass and lit a cigarette.

"Excuse me," he said, resuming his mocking tone. "I believe that I've been taking this buffoonery to seriously. You're right to remind me, my dear. You alone are mistress here, thanks to the god Dollar, and I'm merely your very obedient servant. But tell me, my dear astrologer—if the daughter of Nathan Bering has such a fine sequence in incarnations, can you not enlighten me as to mine?"

Antal Fodor smiled. "No. You'd think that I was exercising bias."

"That doesn't augur anything good. What do you think, Will?"

"I think that all these cocktails aren't as good as a fine bottle. There's the only true nobility! Away with your antique blazons! Only wine has a respectable antiquity."

"Hey now," mocked the Duke, "Don't speak ill of my blazon—it's thanks to that that we're both here. So, Mage Ormus, what eccentricities are there in my anterior incarnations?"

Ormus became momentarily thoughtful. "I can see nothing before the year 1400 of the present era. At that time you were Siwas, an ostler to Macduff, Thane of Glamis. Then one of Lord Talbot's men-at-arms. Afterwards, a barber to George Villiers, Duke of Buckingham. Then one of Queen Anne's cooks. In brief, insignificant individuals. Finally, what you are now."

"That's odd," Shakespeare remarked. "It appears that the spirit doesn't lose its nationality. So you, Mage, have scarcely quit the Orient, and my friend Rutland has remained in Great Britain all the time."

"That's because the soul, on emerging from the body, experiences a very comprehensible fear on sensing itself lost in infinity. Then it returns to Earth and reincarnates preferentially in the country in which it's accustomed to living."

"Come, savant Ormus," said the Duchess, getting to her feet. "Since the Duke doesn't seem to be disposed to occupy himself with you, let's go visit your new apartment and see about the necessary changes."

The Duke got up in order to see Diana out, but he tottered and fell back drunkenly into his armchair. The Duchess, after a scornful glance at her husband, beckoned to the Mage to follow her. As she went past the Duke she put her hand on Ormus' shoulder and said:

"The wife of the Pharaoh Tut-Ankh-Amun, king and god!"

VII. The Philosophy of Sir John Falstaff

Left alone, the two friends looked at one another silently.

"Well, old chap," said Shakespeare, finally, "I think we're checkmated."

"Nothing to be done against that fellow. Did you see? He tamed me like a puppy. It's vexing, all the same, that our will-power escapes us under the influence of another that's superior."

"That's why I didn't persist. He'd have been capable of making me drink water by telling me that it's wine. Pooh!" He rang for the barman, who came in immediately. "A bottle of old port! Come on, George let's have a drink. With this triumphant wine, I'll recover, along with my philosophy of old, my true personality. It's really me who was Shakespeare! Let's drink, damn it!

"Good wine has a double effect. It goes to your head, and dries up all the foolish, stupid and acrid vapors that surround it, renders it sagacious, inventive, full of light, ardent, delectable conceptions, which, transmitted to the tongue, become excellent speeches. The second quality of wine is to reheat the blood, which, cold and sluggish before, left the liver white and pale, which is the symptom of cowardice...

"If you'd had a bottle of this venerable port in your belly, instead of those ignoble cocktails, you'd have stood up to that accursed Mage—may the Devil take him! But no—I think that one's capable of cheating the Devil...

"Come on, old chap, let's drink! That animal's put ice in my blood. Drink! Wine will reheat our interior blood and send it flowing to our extremities, illuminating the face and, like a vivifying fire, giving strength to that entire petty kingdom: the human being.

"Philosophy, my dear friend, is a gold mine guarded by a demon, until wine exploits it and puts it in circulation. Ah! I can feel myself becoming myself again. Here's to you, Roger, to your glory! Drink!"

"Drink!" repeated the Duke, mechanically. "Drink! But why are you calling me Roger?"

"I see you with that forename, Roger Manners, Earl of Rutland. Don't you recognize your old Will?"

"I'd more likely have taken you for that old rogue Falstaff."

"Drink! It will clarify the chaos of ideas for us. The Mage is right. Am I what I appear to be, or am I what I have been? Is it you, Rutland, or me, who is Shakespeare? Why do you claim to have written my plays? It was me, damn it! It's not right that, because you're a gentleman, you can steal my genius."

"Shakespeare!" howled the Duke. "To be or not to be! It's all the same to me. I want my wife!"

"Your wife! Are you mad? Why drag Diana into it? Shame on the man who, with a bottle in front of him, thinks about a woman!"

"Diana!" whimpered the Duke. "I'm used to her. I think I love her—yes, I love her…or rather, I adore her. You hear, Will, I adore her!"

Shakespeare burst out laughing. "Idiot! Do you know what it is to love? I know, me, because I'm a poet. You, love! Poor fool! Poor child!"

"Yes, I know it better than you, wine-bag! Gourd! Barrel! Hogshead!"

"That's all you can find, when you're drinking admirable wine? You're unworthy. You ought to be condemned to drink water. Here, listen and blush with shame. To Love...damn it! My throat's dry and my brain's feeling the effect." He rang. "Fill that up, my old Guild, and listen—you too. Do you know what it is to love? Pour!"

He drank, and remained pensive momentarily.

"To love...to love...is to purchase disdain with tears, modest gazes with heart-rending sighs, a moment's ephemeral joy with twenty nights of sleeplessness and fatigue. In case of conquest, your success will probably be a misfortune; in case of failure, a painful suffering. What's certain is that folly is acquired at the price of reason, or reason vanquished by folly. Well, now, old Guild, go away! You know enough. In your turn, George, what do you say to love?"

"I don't care about love and women. Men have died in all times, but never because of love."

"That's probably true. At any rate, exceptions are rare. To you! Let's leave love to adolescents. Perhaps I've loved—yes, I must have loved...but it was so long ago!"

"Listen! Love is...is... Damn, I had a really profound thought, and pfft!"

"Have a drink! It'll come back. Look, here's your idea. It fell into my glass and drowned. I'll absorb it and it'll spring forth again, as alive and beautiful as antique Venus. Love is the gem and the gum of youth; it has to pour out, or one dies of it. Love is something seductive, tender, subtle, imponderable, a frisson of hope and anxiety; it's the exuberance of sap that rises and buds, then flowers and asks no more than to bear fruit. But love ought to remain in flower, for the fruits of love are children, and children...aren't always amusing. To your health, William...no, that's me, William. No matter. To you!"

"My old Will," stammered George, "you, at least will still be mine, won't you? You'll never leave me, William? My old Shakespeare, you're a sage."

"Not so stupid! Fool I am and fool I shall remain. The role of fool belongs to me, and may the wrinkles of old age give me the strength to laugh. I'm big and fat, but what the hell! Why should a fool with blood in his veins be like a grandfather carved in alabaster? Listen, Rutland—your wife's crazy about this Mage. We'll give up on this New World, which is too pure and too dry for us. Long live Old England! Vive la France! Viva Italia! People know how to live back there. It's time, you see. I'm beginning to get then, and what's worse, to get bitter. Embrace Shakespeare, wretched Rutland! There's nothing worth more than intimate friends, like us."

They hugged one another and, falling on to the carpet, the two drunks went to sleep in one another's arms.

"Love! A word! A word!" snored the Duke, in a dream.

"Drink up!" Shakespeare replied.

VIII. The Empery of the Mage

Preceding Antal Fodor, the Duchess led him to the south wing of Redge House and, assuring him of his possession of it, made a note of the work that had to be done. The Mage took advantage of the opportunity to talk about his master, Adsum.

"That superior old man is my spiritual father. He's my veritable initiator, and almost supernatural intelligence."

"Truly? I'm eager to make his acquaintance."

"I met him six years ago. It was in India, where I was undertaking studies in the origin of religion and the methods used by Yogis to obtain the marvelous results of their prodigies, which are merely a kind of autosuggestion. Adsum revealed in my brain the memory of past incarnations and revealed the mystery of universal life to me."

"What might we not do, the three of us?" cried the Duchess, enthused. "I want to have both of you with me. Draw up a list of all the scientific instruments you need. You mustn't lack anything. You can install a conference-room and a vast laboratory of chemistry and physics on the ground floor, the different services necessary to the propaganda of our religion, the Flower of Truth, on the first floor, and your apartments and an observatory on the second. Don't worry about the expense—I'll take care of everything, and you'll have the right to my gratitude, for I feel that I've revived since I've known you. It seems that the anterior life that you've revealed to me has swollen and filled my being with an exuberant vitality."

"You were asleep; I've awakened you by science, for love."

The Duchess shivered. "For love! That's the first time you've pronounced that word."

"Because you weren't ready—but don't mistake me for a vulgar seeker of amorous adventures. The love that I want from you is a love above humanity: not the sensual love that we've already experienced but the perfect communion of two elite intelligences reigning at a higher level than the sentimental foolishness of our contemporaries like the sun over our globe. It's a love that humans have not yet known—a love, in sum, worthy of us."

Towering over Diana with his greater stature, the Mage plunged his magnificent gaze into the eyes of the new adept, drowning her with its effluvia. Increasingly drawn toward Ormus, subjugated, she fell at his feet and writhed there in a hysterical crisis.

Triumphantly, the Mage considered her, extended at his mercy, imploring him. Then he picked her up and laid her on a chaise-longue. Then, moving his hands through the air above her, he concentrated all the fluidic forces of his being.

"Sleep!" he said. "Sleep, and see!"

Exhausted and motionless, the Duchess was suspended in a previously-unexperienced bliss. It was a strange sensation akin to the intoxication of opium; it seemed to her that her body no longer existed and that the subtle fluid was floating above her own materiality. Everything around her lost massive form to melt into an iridescent fog.

Then, slowly—very slowly—a form, vague at first, became more precise. It consisted of two luminous dots, which became the golden eyes of the Mage Ormus...but a mist thickened, and before the entire body of the prophet, an immaterial body formed, undulating and vaporous: a living and visible fluid. It was like a voluptuous wave poured out by those strange irises of living gold.

Without the Mage ceasing to be visible, the mist brightened gradually; lines stood out, in vivid luminous streaks; the décor took on a more precise aspect.

And she saw...

IX. The Three Visions

Beneath a sky of deep ultramarine, almost violet, scintillating with thousands of stars, a long cortege unfurls between the high columns of an Egyptian palace. On the cedar-wood trusses that support the large slabs of granite forming the roof, the footfalls of another multitude are audible, this one of priests and servants. In accordance with the forbidden rites, they are celebrating the worship of Amon-Ra. Their songs and the muffled noise of zithers and drums reach the depths of the profound corridors.

In response to a signal, innumerable torches of perfumed wax light up, and at the extremity of an upper gallery, two thrones, set on a black granite pedestal, sparkle with all the gold and jewels that decorate them. One the thrones are two hieratic forms—are they human?—with tiaras on their heads: a hawk for the Pharaoh, a phoenix for the Pharaoh's wife.

The cortege files past in silence, depositing at the base of the divine and royal thrones the tithes imposed on everyone. First, between two rows of hoplites armored in bronze, come prisoners of war, chained two by two. As they file past, an Ethiopian giant clad in red and girdled with a triple row of iron scales brands them on the forehead with a red-hot iron. The acrid odor of burnt flesh rises like an incense toward the two monarchs, who do not even blink. Then the prefects of the Empire follow, laden with bags and trays filled with gold and gems or artfully-wrought objects. Then laborers and vine-growers present white staves marked with notches indicating the value of their contributions. The long proces-

69

sion is concluded by embalmers, manufacturers of mortuary bindings and quarrymen working in the hypogea.

Finally, a monstrous figure appears: a colossal mannequin in which porters are hidden. It represents Amentet, the goddess of Death, a mummy circled with black strips of cloth, on which the goddess's commandments are traced in red letters. The head, coiffed in a pschent, is that of a she-wolf with flamboyant eyes and a yawning maw. When it arrives in front of the thrones, the mannequin folds up, until the head is level with the Pharaoh's feet; a tongue emerges, which licks the king's feet; then the monster goes around the double throne and disappears.

The crowd is arranged to either side in the galleries. Suddenly, dancers surge forth from behind the altar; the figures engraved on the columns are animated, and mingle with the ballerinas, who then mime the mystery of Isis and Osiris.

At the height of grandiose spectacle, two hands—those of Ormus—settle on the heads of the Pharaoh and his wife, tipping them backwards. Then the sleeper recognizes, in the Pharaoh, Antal Fodor, and in his wife, her own image. Perfumed clouds rise up among the dancers. The torches pale, and everything is effaced and transformed.

The Nile unfurls its blue waves beneath a moonlight that tints the obelisks and pylons of the temples of Luxor and Karnak with a pink gleam. Over the river, which resembles a long stream of lily-white mercury, glides a trireme with three ranks of oarsmen. The oars, maneuvered rhythmically, scarcely brush the surface of the waves, which they furrow with flamboyant streaks. A gentle and harmonious music gives rhythm to the oarsmen's movements.

From time to time, voices rise up, clearer and more vibrant than the voices of women: the voices of the castrate servants of the temple of Thoth. They are singing a melancholy love-song. Ahead of the frolicsome vessel, an entire procession of swimmers creates the illusion of sirens guiding the ship with silken cords garnished with flowers and foliage.

The air is embalmed; the entire landscape respires quietude. The river is so broad that both its banks are lost in a roseate mist, from which emerge the vague silhouettes of palm-trees and laurier-roses.

Who is that woman lying on the deck, almost nude, on a heap of splendid cushions, whose sapphire silk seems to be competing with the waters of the nourishing river? That divinity, rather, for everyone prostrates themselves before her, is Queen Cleopatra, the mistress of the triumvir Mark Antony…and it is Diana Bering.

Cleopatra, on this night of repose between two orgies, has left the protector of Egypt in Alexandria to take care of affairs of State, and she is going up the Nile, simultaneously soothing her depression and her reverie.

But a terrible cry causes the indolent woman to start. A swimmer has just been seized by a crocodile, which is dragging its prey away in the midst of a cloud of foam. Interested, Cleopatra watches.

The frightened swimmers try to climb aboard, but in response to a gesture, the galley's overseers drive them back with whiplashes. Cleopatra, leaning on her elbow, watches, hoping for a further attack—but silence reigns again.

The nonchalant woman sighs. A luminous mist surrounds her, in which the golden eyes of the Mage float over Cleopatra, and everything disappears.

Now, other images:
Her, still—but this time, clad in ample silks, rigid and brittle. A heavy dalmatic hemmed with broad gold embroidery weighs upon her shoulders; a tiara, aureoled with diamonds, weighs upon her forehead; she is crushed beneath that magnificent pomp. Around her, an entire prostrated court is only waiting for a gesture of her hand to satisfy her slightest desire. Diana Bering recognizes herself again.

She is in Byzantium, and that immense hall with the columns and the cupola covered with gold-limned paintings is the basilica of Saint Sophia. What is she doing, then, on that platform, isolated by a splendid tapestry from the rest of the church? She has become a Christian. It is a new religion, fraternal and barbaric, in which people quibble over words.

An old man clad in white has just appeared on an elevated pulpit. He preached, his gestures seemingly menacing. She recalls that it is the patriarch John, who has merited the surname Chrysostom—golden-tongued—and Diana is the divine Eudoxia, the wife of the Emperor Arcadius. She has wanted to hear the preacher, and, with a smile of disdain permanently upon her lips, she is amusing herself greatly to see that old ape, sweating and dusty, fulminating vehemently against her.

What to the priest's curses matter to her? Eudoxia has only to lift a finger to crush him. What force he imposes upon her, though! The madman reminds the nobles of the earth, in his homily, that they are no more before the Eternal than insects crawling in the grass. That poor rhetorical image causes laughter to break out. The insect is him!

John Chrysostom has heard the insulting laughter, and he pronounces an anathema against Omnipotence. This time, he gets carried away. The Empress rises to hear feet and leaves the cathedral. All the nobles, their servants and their vassals follow her majestic example, attentive to being noticed, in order that the Augusta will know who her faithful followers are.

And Chrysostom is left in the church alone.

Outside, in the blinding light, an entire terrorized people acclaims the triumphant woman, who, borne on a magnificent litter, returns to her imperial palace, tried and annoyed. What an idea, to go out in this stifling heat to hear that graybeard criticize her dissolute mores!

Oof! She is back inside; she is free. Finally relieved of her sumptuous vestments, naked, sprawling on a silken bed, she sends for ballerinas and actors. But someone with a pale face, drags himself languidly toward her couch, supported by a vigorous soldier. It is the Emperor Arcadius, the Iberian, come to exhaust his last strength in an orgy.

She looks at him, and sees that livid mask gradually brighten, the dull, dead eyes animate and shine. But why has her adversary, that John Chrysostom, come to disturb the feast, to thunder once again against the new Herodias, the new Jezebel? And why does Chrysostom himself evoke, in this vision, the venerable Adsum, who she only knows as yet through the words of the Mage she loves—Adsum, whose eyes are resplendent and whose mouth is full of invective?

X. A Patrician Household

Someone knocked gently on the door of the boudoir. Mary O'Brien came in.

"It's me, dear. I've come from New York. I've seen Pytor, and I'm bringing the first article."

"Ah," said the Duchess, getting up. As if to bring herself back to reality, she made a few swift tours of the room.

"What's the matter? You were asleep—did I wake you up?"

"No, I was just daydreaming. Let's see the article." She scanned the newspaper rapidly. "Very good! Very good! It's written by a man convinced of the truth. The Mage will be satisfied."

"I ran into the Duke. He wants to see you."

The Duchess frowned. After a moment, reflection, however, she said: "Well, let him in, Mary—but you can stay. I need to talk to you, and the Duke won't be here long."

The Irishwoman went out and came back with the Duke. The fumes of the wine having dissipated, his face was a trifle shriveled, his complexion paler and his nose redder, but there was no other trace of drunkenness. He kissed his wife's hand and let himself fall into an armchair. Mary had retired to a corner and picked up a book. Unconstrained and alert, the Duke did not appear to have retained any memory of what had been said in Antal Fodor's presence.

"I believe, my dear, that given our social situation, we ought to begin the season and hold the first party. What do you say to a big dinner followed by a costumed ball? Something in the spirit of the day—naturalism, exceedingly realistic. For example, burglars and hotel-thieves, all in black, and morphine addicts. It would be amusing, for millionaires, to dress up as riff-raff."

"No, ridiculous. Can you see me as a hotel-thief or a low-class prostitute?"

"Do you have another idea?"

"Yes—a party in the style of the Pharaoh Tut-Ankh-Amun."

Rutland concealed a grimace. "Bravo! That's a good idea—but that epoch requires a rather complicated decoration."

"Your collaboration would not be unwelcome."

"At your orders, my darling. You know that I'm always eager to be agreeable to you. Some years ago, Shakespeare and I went to an antique fête organized in Paris by the Quat'z'Arts. In that masked ball—a reconstitution in accordance with a book, *L'Orgie Latine*[14]—Messalina appeared stark naked, on a litter borne by gladiators, acclaimed by senators, tribunes, Roman soldiers, Gauls, Greeks, Libyans and Parthians. There was Emperor Claudius, misshapen and stammering, the Consul Silius, the Empress's favorite, animal-tamers of all sorts, and courtesans as naked as roses. It was delightful!"

"Mine will be even better—although I won't be dressed like your Messalina."

"Oh, you'd look very good in the nude."

"You flatter me. I hope that we'll be ready for early December. You can advertise the party, so that everyone can prepare their costumes. Send William to me. He ought to have some good advice for that sort of party."

---

[14] Champsaur's 1903 novel; his most successful book.

"Don't worry, the rascal's competent. You don't have any special instructions for me?"

"No, I'll leave it to you—I have to talk to Mary."

The Duke got up, kissed his wife's hand again and left, reassured, for the moment, on the subject of the separation. "Bah! One doesn't renounce being the Duchess of Rutland just like that."

And with that armistice, the Duke of Rutland rejoined the joyful Shakespeare in the forbidden bar.

XI. Between Two Mages

The installation of Adsum and Ormus at Redge House took place discreetly. With the support of abundant dollars, the fitting out of the various rooms was organized very rapidly. In two weeks, the laboratory, the scientific instruments and the observatory were in place and ready for use. In the offices, four stenographers were relentlessly typing the propaganda of the new religion, the Flower of Truth.

The Mage Ormus and Diana animated all this activity, and in between times, occupied themselves with the preparations for the party. A feverish movement, therefore, reigned throughout the house. Only Adsum worked apart, not involving himself with the party or the publicity. He was not inactive, however; he was the inexhaustible spring from which Antal Fodor extracted the documentation of the new faith.

The Father arrived at Redge House by night, not wanting to compromise his prestige by donning a modern costume. The first time Diana saw him, he was clad in his ample white robe, his long hair contained within a golden circlet; she had the impression of being confronted by a kind of Merlin, unvictimized by any Viviane.

The old man assessed the billionairess with a single glance. He understood immediately the use that he and his pupil could make of her. Not that he judged Diana Bering to be a fool—far from it. In the environment in which she had lived, however, the complete satisfaction of all her whims, thanks to the great god Dollar, had given her an exceptional ennui.

Diana was not vain—vanity does not exist in the United States—but a kind of indifference to enjoyment rendered her immense fortune worthless, and satiety brings disgust. It is a kind of justice that those for whom everything is possible no longer desire anything. It was, therefore, very fortunate for that idler without an appetite for anything to have encountered the two mages. In orientating hr mind toward a new world, they were restoring a mental activity to her life, which, by virtue of lassitude, had been lacking for a long time.

Psychic contact with the handsome Mage awoke previously unknown sensations in the woman. It is not in vain that one suggests to a woman that she has been the wife of a Pharaoh, Cleopatra and Eudoxia—which is to say, the triumph of Oriental luxury. The beautiful female animal that Diana was excited herself with an equivocal lust; it required all the imposing coldness of Ormus for the American woman not to have thrown herself into his arms as yet.

The two mages reasoned soundly in fearing that the woman's sexual intoxication might harm her mystical initiation. Sometimes, Ormus too sensed desire heating up his young loins, but the habit he had contracted among the fakirs of taming the beast in order to arrive at spiritual concentration permitted him to resist temptation.

Adsum said to his adept: "It's absolutely necessary that the woman's mind should be ours. Afterwards, the body will come, without too much risk to our plans—and then again, men of our worth ought not to be vulgar prostitutes. It's necessary that the billions should be the common property of the three of us, without desire on our part or regret on hers.

The Duchess addressed Ormus as "my Master" and Adsum as "my Father"—a nuance that indicated the veneration inspired by the two scientists.

All three came together in the immense room converted into a laboratory of the psychic sciences; sprawled in comfortable rocking chairs, they swayed gently, while the Father explained the fundamentals of universal life to Diana.

"Since human thought has abandoned religious mythologies in order to search for scientific realities, people, moved by their curiosity to know, their need to penetrate the great mystery, have launched forth into hypotheses as fantastic as the priests' absurdities. The pride people feel in being among the beings—the only ones, they believe—able to transmit thought and to exercise judgment on what they see, carries them away and makes them overshoot the target. We are ignorant with regard to the formation of worlds and our minds are not yet sufficiently developed to comprehend that enigma.

"Why are these millions of Suns traveling through the universe, dragging with them other worlds of invisible planets? Why, on these wandering globes, are there innumerable humankinds, which are doubtless different from ours? Why that exuberance of lives, replicated on the surface of every heavenly body? Science has suppressed the divinity because of the impossibility of comprehending it. Certainly, the gods of human creation do not stand up to sane judgment; they reflect the faults and vices of the creature too accurately; the scant virtue with which humans have endowed them renders them useless, and even injurious, to humankind. Is it necessary, for that reason, to deny all creative intelligence? It is a serious matter. Does it or does it not exist?

"When we see so many marvels around us, so much animal humanity around our individual humanity, it is permissible to doubt that it is merely the result of physical laws. And if it were, that would prove nothing, since he laws similarly demand an inventor. It required millions of centuries for humans, the latest stage of terrestrial humanity, to begin to suspect a little of the truth. What does the future have in store for us? Before the death of the Earth, will the superhuman appear? That is what we dare not affirm, but that is what it is our duty to attempt. Failure is possible, for we know that other civilizations have collapsed without the superhuman appearing.

"It does not matter. In the universe, time does not exist; a second and a century have the same value. In the same way, in nature, insects—what am I saying? infusoria, microbes—are beings as complete as humans, but their thought differs so much from ours that we do not understand them. All atoms, insects, birds, quadrupeds and humans, have as their primary need the propagation of the species, and the more inferior a being seems, the greater is its fecundity. After propagation is nourishment; and humans, so superior in their intelligence, are forced to sacrifice to these two needs under pain of physical and mental degeneration.

"We see animals devouring one another, and conclude a supremacy in ourselves that is false, since we only conserve out existence to the determinant of those of plants and animals, not to mention futile wars. Some people do not eat flesh, believing that they do not have a right to kill, but they make no bones about killing the plants that are the principle of flesh, since they are flesh in preparation. Given this principle, that everything that is lives, and that, on our globe, everything lives—

transformation being life—it is the duty of the Thinker to extend that viewpoint to the planet, from the planet to the Suns, and from the Suns to the splendid life of all the heavenly bodies.

"Everything is connected, everything is similar. The atom that divides to give birth to another is as complete in its species as the animals that seem superior to it. Let us add to the formidable quantity of beings existing on our Earth those which live within ourselves as well as in other beings, and let us ask ourselves whether this planet that bear us might also have its soul, a creative will, in order that everything that is, should be?

"And that myriad of other beings of every form, of every color, of so many kinds—are they useful? Evidently not. Twenty types would have sufficed for general alimentation. What do humans need in order to live? Oxen, wheat, wine—and that is already superabundance, since other creatures have but one invariable aliment. Why, then, that infinity of creatures? Is it the pastime of a Creator seeking a distraction in the variety of species, as the assembly of words expresses thousands of ideas for us?

"A Provençal, the entomologist Fabre, has devoted his life to the study of insects in the fields of his farm, and one remains wonderstruck at the aspect of all those very tiny mentalities; some have a prescience of what their children, their successors, will be and do, and prepare special nourishment for the day on which they will partake of existence. What is human intelligence, so long in formation, compared with these minuscule ones, which only have a brief existence but are able to prepare so well for their descendants? That is the proof that the notion of time does not exist in nature. Some ephemera, which only live for a day, might perhaps have a duration as full as that of a oak five or six hundred years old.

"What language do oaks speak, and poplars in the wind? How do ants understand one another? Instinct, people say. In humans, instinct is in competition with the mind. So be it—but it is still that part, the instinct, that guides. We attribute a vitality to plants, but not instinct. Why not? Does the plant not have the intelligence to prepare its seed for reproduction, and sometimes, to associate itself with insects or the wind as a means of transportation? Woe to the mute! A plant does not have the right to intelligence, or even to instinct; however, it exists, it breathes, it is happy, it suffers, it lives, it acts—which is to say, it is transformed.

"For me, everything has a soul, and universal life extends from atoms to planets, each of which has its particular thought processes and its own intelligence, in its course through the universe, describing uninterrupted spirals, undertaking its career as a planet in a manner indecipherable to us, thus far, but which is a way of life, as is human life.

"Life! That is the great mystery, and death does not exist. Everything is transformed, but nothing dies. But life—*why?* With what end? We have been subject to numerous incarnations, and yet, we're still humans. Some, like us, are making intellectual progress, but have we any assurance that the progress in question will continue? The genius that has been able to acquire the supreme instruction—which is to say, the sum of human knowledge—must, to maintain its progress, escape the everyday, in order that its liberated spirit, fluid, subtle and imponderable, might float through the universe in search of another world, where beings more intelligence than itself understand more, and from step to step, rise all the way to what we call by that incomprehensible word God."

"Then you're not brining certainty," Diana exclaimed, "but doubt?"

"To doubt is, for the human mind, to be making progress. It is better to say 'I don't know' than to propagate errors. But consider the fluids! We have found applications for them before formulating the rules that govern them. The fluids are nothing, and that nothing is everything. The initiate can constrain it to be a force that we employ in order to impose our will, nothing and everything, of which we have not yet been able to analyze the causes

"My psychic fluid can influence an inferior will, can annihilate it or multiply it tenfold, giving astonishing results. But the human brain, that prodigious accumulator, is paltry by comparison with the fluidic forces of the Earth. Perhaps, in a few years, the fluidic forces will replace electricity, as that has replaced steam. What will come after the fluidic forces? Perhaps the Soul of the Earth will yield some of its amazing secrets to us. The souls of planets, the souls of suns, are mysterious figures, of which the Unknowable is perhaps the number."

Adsum stopped talking, and everyone was pensive.

Ormus finally broke the silence. "When, thanks to you, Master, I perceived the mystery of reincarnation, and, remounting the scale of past centuries, I believed, in an extraordinary excitement, that I was one of the elect, I acquired—alas!—only one certainly: the futility of death. But if there is, in that knowledge of the past, a means of domination over others, that prideful sentiment does not satisfy me, Father. To be a leader of men and woman is a sad profession—but there is no objective above and beyond that."

"To be at the head of a multitude of the ignorant, my son, is undoubtedly degrading for the leader. A fine business to rule over imbeciles! We, on the contrary, Ormus, aspire to reign over the intellectual elite, and from that mass of intelligences, enlightenment might spring forth."

"O Father, who can surpass you?" exclaimed the Duchess.

"My son, Ormus. He is young; he has been able to profit from my science, and he has long years ahead of him. Alas, a human life is too short, and so many superior minds allow themselves to be drawn away from study by the pride of seeming greater than they really are. Only detachment from all vanities can lead to the truth."

"In that case, my Father, you must disapprove of the Egyptian fête we're preparing?"

"No, Daughter, for it will bring us new adepts. It is one of the shameful aspects of our work, to be obliged to make a noise in order to attract and command attention, but even God has need of advertisement: of priests, cathedrals, temple, churches and bell-towers."

XI. Preparations for the Party

There was a vast lawn in front to Redge House, and the Duchess had decided that the Egyptian fête would be held there, in winter, thanks to the construction of an immense greenhouse. The gardeners took up expanses of grass and large trees, and subterranean heaters warmed the enormous area. The colossal hothouse occupied the entire length of the façade, the summer gardens having to serve for the arrival of the gusts and their automobiles. The iron pylons supporting the glazed roof, lined with decorated stucco, were reminiscent of the grandiose colonnades of Karnak.

In the midst of this intense activity, the Duke of Rutland and his shadow, the stout Shakespeare, were wandering back and forth chatting.

"I'll give the Egyptian fête credit for the amusement there is in preparing it," said Will, "inasmuch as the Duchess, entirely devoted to her psychic studies, scarcely pays any heed to it and is leaving it to us. What do you think of the other one, Adsum?"

"Cut from same cloth as the young mage, and sturdier. Between those two doctors, my wife can't resist, so I shan't get in the way of her plans. I might as well try to stop the sun. Close the door on a woman's mind and it'll escape through the window; close the window and it'll fly up the chimney, with the smoke it resembles."

"Yes, but all the dust of this construction-yard is giving me a thirst."

"You don't say! Will, don't you think that obelisk would look better if it were more isolated? But here comes the Duchess—with Ormus, naturally."

"You're not jealous?" The Duke shook his head. "Man of the world, eh! You were born with a money-bag where your heart ought to be."

"And you with a sponge, you old soak."

"That' my heart, pieced by the thousand arrows of the malign god that have reduced it to that state. Hey, I've got an idea! I'll ask the Mage who is the most amorous of the three of us, to see what he'll say in front of your wife."

"You're mad! You'll make an enemy of the Duchess."

"If fools can't talk about the follies that sane folk commit, I'll hand in my resignation."

The two men went over to Ormus and the Duchess, who were watching the work in progress from the top of the front steps.

"O Mage, my handsome Mage," sang William, "what news have you brought us?"

"It seems to me that everything is going well, Master Will."

"And your charming pupil?" Shakespeare continued, bowing to Diana. "She believes in science and in sagacity, as in beauty. Permit me, Madame, to ask a question of the Mage. We have three men here, if you will do me the honor of still considering me as one. Which of us is the most amorous?"

"Will, Will," said the Duke, "you're embarking on a dangerous passage."

Rutland changed the subject by drawing the Duchess's attention to a detail of the decoration and drawing her toward the obelisk, leaving the Mage alone with Will.

"You have a great deal of intelligence, Mr. Shakespeare. Can't you apply it more seriously? There's too great a depth of wisdom in your Epicurean philosophy for you to consider my presence here as a danger to your friend. Don't waste your time with epigrams—it would be the contest of the earthenware pot against the iron pot. There are fatalities against which it's better not to struggle."

"I know—and you're one of those fatalities. You think it interesting to penetrate the secrets of nature. It's an occupation like any other. Personally, I think it's futile, and that nothing will come out of all this occult nonsense, including your fluidic science, from the viewpoint of the mystery of life and death. What's the point? The carcass of William the Fool will leave behind a skull as empty as that of the handsome Ormus. As for our situation here, you're a parasite like me, but you're the strongest, and certainly the cleverest, of the three of us. Be indulgent to George and me—leave us a bone."

The Duke returned with Diana. "Well, are you two sages squabbling?"

"There is always agreement between those in love with beauty."

"That lyricism is a mask for your intelligence. Don't fight us, Mr. Shakespeare. And you, Master, let's go back in. We'll discuss less futile questions with our Father."

XIII. A Party at Tut-Ankh-Amun's

"It's more than marvelous," said Robert Molly, the wealthy owner of large International Hotels, "it's magical—and I reckon that Diana Bering's spent five million dollars."

"What a foolish mania you have for calculating prices, my dear! It's splendid, that's all."

"But I have to make calculations my dear. Won't it be necessary for us to throw a party too? So..."

At that moment, Molly and his wife were approached by a magnificent Egyptian lord, followed by two gigantic soldiers: Thebans with torsos circled in bronze, coiffed with hawk's-head helmets. It was John Flatsbury and his sons, Ralph and David.

"Well!" said Papa Flatsbury. "Old Bering's daughter is putting on quite a show!"

For all the Yankees, the Duchess of Rutland was still Nathan Bering's daughter. The Duke was universally considered to be a luxury accessory to which the American billionairess had treated herself. For Americans, the antiquity of a name has no importance, and the nobilities of the Old World are considered as the descendants of brigands and toadies rather than national glories.

The group passed between the pylons of the temple and climbed the flight of steps giving access to the colonnade. Then, turning round, they contemplated the ensemble of the decoration.

At their feet was an immense quadrangular plaza, whose gigantic columns terminated in lotus-flower surrounds. Those columns, ornamented with symbolic figures, opened on all sides to perspectives of panoramic paintings, forming a perfect illusion. Here were the banks of the Nile, there the temples of Luxor, and further away, Thebes, its palaces and its temples.

Even further away, between two rows of columns, which colossal mirrors reflected to infinity, was a further panorama: Philae and its temple, with the first cataract. There, a long avenue of palm-trees injected a hint of verdure, framing the view of the island and the temple of Isis. Through clumps of laurier-roses, the cataract was visible, given life by a thin trickle of water, running incessantly. A narrow basin beneath received the fall, and, by means of a skillfully-obtained effect, gave the illusion of the majestic Nile.

Between other columns, there were other panoramas: on one side, the desert, with the Sphinx and the pyramids of Giza, illuminated with a blue and pink glow by a beautiful African night. Under the colonnades the lighting changed; thousands of electric lights simulated lamps and torches.

Behind Molly and his wife, in the room of the feast, hundreds of slaves were setting up and laying tables lined with narrow brass beds. The elevated room would permit the guests to see dancers and acrobats while eating and drinking. A decoration of columns and pylons masked Redge House completely.

The crowd was numerous; New York had fought over the invitations, and everyone was competing in the splendor of their costumes, copied from the beautiful processions engraved on the walls of the temple of Luxor.

Diana, her head coiffed in a royal pschent representing a jeweled golden phoenix, whose extended wings descended over her shoulders, had a veritable majesty, seated at the end of a colonnade on a throne of jasper and ivory, whose arms were golden sphinxes with eyes of beryl. By her side, the Duke, as a Pharaoh, cut a rather paltry figure. Made-up and bronzed, with a black wig under his royal pschent, he had painted his eyebrows and lips.

Only two guests created a stain in that brilliant Egypt: William Shakespeare, as an actor of the Elizabethan era, and Charlie Chaplin, in his habitual costume, with wide trousers, a tight-fitting jacket, his cane and his immense worn-out boots. The celebrated comic was too sure of his success to sacrifice it to an ancient costume that would have rendered him unrecognizable.

The crowd had arrived at about ten o'clock. Charlie hid his admiration beneath grimaces and bewildered expressions, which made the grave and sumptuous Egyptians writhe with laughter.

"That animal Chaplin is spoiling the illusion for us," said Pytor. "But for him. I'd begin to believe that it was real."

"Oho! Look—here comes the real Pharaoh."

"But that's the mage, Antal Fodor."

"He's heading for the throne. My God! I wouldn't want to be in Rutland's shoes. He looks bad beside Ormus."

"And who's the other one—the old man?" asked Chaplin. "One might think he was the Eternal Father."

Meanwhile, the mage Ormus, splendidly costumed as a Pharaoh, coiffed with a hawk's-head tiara, went forward. Beside him, as the high priest of Helios, was Adsum, clad in white and gold lamé, with a diadem studded with precious stones over his long hair. They were both marching without affectation, simple and magnificent.

Having arrived before the throne, Ormus climbed the steps and, with an irresistible gesture, signaled to the Duke to surrender his place. Nonplussed, the latter hesitated—but, subjugated by the magnificent gaze, he stood up and stood aside.

Diana had got up. Standing, with his arms folded over his chest, the Pharaoh, motionless in a hieratical pose, seemed a colossus of granite. Diana, with a truly regal gesture, placed her hand on the Pharaoh's shoulder, while Adsum, his arms majestically raised, seemed to be summoning celestial blessings upon the imperial couple.

And Charlie Chaplin said: "Look! That takes the biscuit!"

The Duke hesitated momentarily; he tried to fight that imperative influence, but he did not have sufficient will-power in his overly superficial mind. He retreated from a brawl that would have cost him not only his wife but his fortune. He went down the steps of the throne and, joining Shakespeare, drew away with him, pretending to be laughing at something the other had said to him. The triumphant Mage remained immobile in his hieratic pose next to the Pharaoh's wife, accepting the consequences of that domination.

The crowd, mildly astonished at first, yielded to the impression of the moment and the milieu. Charlie, in his grotesque costume, advanced to the foot of the throne and, with an admiring grimace, testified with twirls of his crooked cane to his exuberant enthusiasm. There was a long outburst of laughter, and then frenetic exclamations.

A suggestive fluid emanated from the three principal actors, imposing itself to such a degree that everyone believed, momentarily, that they were contemporaries of ancient Egypt. Then, returning to reality, they applauded once again the defection of the Duke—that English aristocrat who brought a kind of luster to their young democracy but whom, deep down, they scorned as a useless individual.

A distraction was required in order that the scene should not become embarrassing. Adsum made a gesture; immediately, emerging from a gallery hidden behind the throne, a group of fearsome warriors in scaled breastplates and helmets simulating the heads of lions spread out to either side in two ranks, clearing the area intended for the dancers. Then came a troupe of musicians carrying large semicircular harps, zithers, tall drums in the form of brass-bound barrels, cymbals and long trumpets with funnels shaped like dragons' heads took their places facing the throne. Then a whole flock of young and nimble dancing-girls leapt out, whirling momentarily before freezing in adoring poses in front of the Pharaoh and the Pharaoh's wife.

Adsum had gone to take his place behind the two sovereigns, and suddenly, behind them, a large golden disk rose, radiating fulgurant electric flames. On the disk, the symbol of the new religion, the rejuvenated cult of the divine Helios, the Sun God, shone letters of fire, which read:

The Flower of Truth

With a single, admirably rhythmic movement, the dancers, extending their arms toward the Pharaoh, bowed down adoringly. With three vibrant chords, the antique orchestra struck up, first a slow and monotonous chant, and then became gradually more animated, amalgamating the dirge with brilliant poems orchestrated by Saint-Saëns, Félicien David and Vincent d'Indy. Cheers and enthusiastic whistles came from all directions, like rockets. Then, when the ballet concluded, the dancers arranged themselves in a harmonious border, like veritable flowers of flesh, and an entire phalanx of clowns and acrobats flooded the floor, all in swarthy and striped leotards, coiffed with Egyptian pschents.

Beneath the galleries, broad steps permitted the spectators to see effortlessly and without fatigue. Greek and Nubian slaves had brought masses of multicolored cushions, and everyone was able to sit down as they pleased. That disposition avoided the monotony of spectators seated in a regular manner, as in a theater.

"Hang on," said William—who, installed on a pile of cushions on the top step, was enjoying the extraordinary fête sybaritically. "Where's your wife?"

"What?" said Rutland.

At the most gripping moment of an acrobatic exercise, when all gazes were fixed on the artistes, the double throne had pivoted, turning on its axis, and had disappeared behind the enormous golden disk, which was now on its own, sparkling and radiating:

The Flower of Truth

The Duke remained momentarily nonplussed.

"I believe, my dear chap," said Shakespeare, phlegmatically, that if you haven't been cuckolded yet, you soon will be."

"Can't be helped! But I look ridiculous in this costume, and for supper, I'm going to put on my smoking jacket. You'll do likewise, I suppose?"

"Why? I'm fine like this; I'm in keeping with my name."

"Finally! Are you coming?"

XIV. The Two Pharaohs

In sum, Diana had never loved, and her temperament, rather cool, had not yet opened up in liaisons that had only brought her more banality rather than the pleasure for which she had hoped. In spite of her real beauty, her compatriots only saw her as a billionairess, the daughter of Nathan Bering, and Europeans as a rich golden fleece to be conquered. Diana's youth had passed between these respects and appetites, but now, with her thirties, a need for enjoyment had come—and that hope lit up her youth. Antal Fodor was unique; he had awakened veritable desire in her, and inspired the advertisement of love. Exacerbated by the dreams of her anterior existences, she could no longer think about anything but their realization.

They were both sitting on a large divan in one of the lateral rooms, tightly enlaced. The Mage was speaking.

"O my spouse! My ideal and real wife! Beauty who reveals herself more alive and les immaterial with every passing hour, I love you! I love you madly. At first I loved you like a sister in election, the one of whom my soul dreamed, the sister of my mind and my faith—but now I admire you with mortal eyes, which enumerate all your charms, and now, I am merely a man."

"No, you're my god: the one for whom I was waiting, in order to know the truth…and a love as powerful as the universal force."

"Diana, my soul is upon your body, with all the caresses that my hands, my lips, my eyes and all my senses combined can find. And this indissoluble union consecrates a love such as no human before us has known. And, Beauty of all Beauties, I shall list the details your beauty, in order that the sound of my words shall make you know your value and your treasures: your divine eyes, where mine lose themselves, as in an ocean; your lips, where I collect, with your breath, all the perfumes of gardens; your neck, more supple and whiter than a swan's. And I, for whom antique sensualities are no secret, will initiate you into the sublime immodesties of the masters of the amorous sciences of India, Egypt and Rome. O my mistress, I love you! O my wife, I adore you!"

And the Mage drew the Pharaoh's wife toward him, and took a devouring kiss from her lips.

Intoxicated by that fiery caress, Diana, her nerves taut in a paroxysm of passion, squeezed him frantically in her arms, and swooned convulsively under the ardent caress.

"Oh, I beg your pardon," said a mocking voice. "Am I disturbing you?"

Ormus turned round. On the threshold of the little room, the Mage perceived the Duke of Rutland and Shakespeare.

"My compliments," the Duke continued, taking a step forward. "You're very skilled in all the arts. Once again, I beg your pardon—and don't imagine that I was spying on you. I came back in to take off this Pharaoh costume, in which I feel ridiculous, and it was sheer chance that caused me to happen upon you. I'll go."

In the Mage's arms, momentarily confused, Diana opened her eyes again. She saw the Duke beating a retreat.

"What is it?"
"Nothing," said Ormus.

"The Duke of Rutland! It's necessary to get rid of that clown—tomorrow!"

Meanwhile, followed by Will, the Duke went back to his apartment. When they were in the Duke's bedroom, Shakespeare laughed.

"Here you are, then, as in the soldiers' song, the *chef de gare*."[15]

Rutland strode back and forth across the room, while taking off his Pharaoh costume. "I believe, old Will, that we won't be staying in the United States much longer."

"And I'm glad of it. Drinking in hiding takes away the pleasure. Then again, that sorcerer's putting ideas in my head, and the women are expensive here. If you didn't have me, my poor George, what would become of you?"

The Duke rang. A manservant came in.

"Have a bottle of champagne sent up, and come back to help me dress."

William picked up the scattered pieces of the Pharaoh costume and threw them all in a corner.

"Tell me, George, do you think your presence is indispensable to the party? Let's leave the sorcerer to his Pharaoh's wife, so long as he pleases her. In this masquerade we look like a couple of imbeciles. These mak-

---

[15] The reference is to a song popular in the trenches during the Great War, known simply *"la chanson du chef du gare"* [the station-master song] whose refrain was *"il est cocu le chef de gare"* [he's cuckolded the station-master]; its theme was subsequently recycled—long after 1929—into the much more elegant Jacques Ferrat/Guy Thomas song *"Le chef de gare est amoureux,"* which is now far better known.

ers of millions regard us as old English wrecks. There's a fine supper waiting down below, but I'll stay here with you, until the end."

"You're being an idiot, my dear chap."

"No, in my head there's intelligence, like fire in a stone, but it's necessary to strike it lightly with a good bottle."

During this conversation the Duke had put on a pajama-suit, and the two friends sat down with the bottle of champagne.

"The party fills me with melancholy," Rutland said, in a slurred voice. "Why do people cling to existence? Our best repose is sleep, but we have an exaggerated fear of death, which resembles it, even though we're only made of atoms issued from dust. Will, it's not being cuckolded that afflicts me—it's having been a lousy Pharaoh.!

"As to that, old chap, yes; beside the other, you did look bad."

"Swine!" groaned the Duke. It was unclear whether the epithet was addressed to Will or Ormus.

Then Rutland slumped back in his armchair and went to sleep.

Shakespeare emptied his glass and looked at his friend. "You're getting old, George; you're getting old."

He shook his head, and was subsiding into his armchair when he heard a distant storm of cheers and the sound of trumpets.

"Too bad! I'm going back down. I'll make George's excuses." And after a glance in a mirror, Shakespeare, as fresh as a rose, went down to supper.

XV. Dream or Reality?

The trumpet-blast that had shaken away Shakespeare's melancholia was the signal for supper. As for the cheers, they were addressed to the two Amphitryons, Diana and Ormus, who came at the head of a cortege of important functionaries and military leaders to guide the crowd to the feast. In spite of the number of guests, there was room for everyone. Butlers in antique dress, like all the staff, hastened to seat everyone. Diana took her place, with the Mage Ormus and the high priest Adsum at her sides.

The Pharaoh's table was elevated by three steps and occupied the center of the immense room. To either side, in two rows, were smaller tables for the guests. With only a few exceptions—guests who got carried away—there was an unavoidable anachronism; people sat down in the fashion of modern civilization. The service was also bang up to date, for everyone's convenience. To eat lying on a triclinium, serving oneself one-handed, with no knife or fork, would have discomfited many people.

At the Pharaoh's table the intimates of Redge House were gathered—including, naturally, the parasites William Shakespeare and Mary O'Brien. Mary had manifested a great repugnance to her protectress, who had forced her to comply. She was wearing the loincloth and violet-bordered black veil of a priestess of Isis.

Diana frowned. Two places at the table remained empty: the Duke's and William's. Charlie Chaplin, seeing an opportunity for buffoonery, advanced and sat down unceremoniously opposite the Pharaoh's wife. He turned his hat over and over with an embarrassed expression, and finally stuck it on the head of a nearby Nubian slave. Diana looked at him askance, but he was examining the Pharaoh's wife with such an ingenuously idiotic expression that she ended up bursting into laughter.

Young Colonel Charles Lindbergh was in stitches. In spite of his deification, for having crossed the Atlantic in an airplane a few months earlier, he had only added human wings, invented by others,[16] to the brain and lungs of a bird, with its instinct of direction. Nevertheless, he was a hawk-headed Egyptian god.

At that joyful moment, Shakespeare arrived. He approached the sovereign, in spite of protocol, and whispered a few words in her ear. Her Majesty shrugged her shoulders and smiled disdainfully.

"So much the better," she said. "So much the better."

"What's up?" asked Charlie, comically.

"Nothing serious. My husband sends his excuses. The fête has tired him out; he's resting in his apartment."

"Good night, Milord!" the clown exclaimed. "You see, Milady, that I did well to take his place. At table only, alas!"

For everyone, Lord Rutland was merely an accessory, and his absence had no effect on the general gaiety. To begin with, discreet music accompanied the first courses. In spite of the dry regime, or perhaps because of

---

[16] This is a sly reference to Champsaur's novel *Les Ailes de l'homme* [Human Wings] (1917 but revised by necessity, having been written before the outbreak of the war; tr. as *The Human Arrow*), about a transatlantic crossing by air. The original version was restored, with a new and much briefer addendum, for reissue a few weeks after Lindbergh's flight.

it, Cyprus and Shiraz wines ran in floods. Charlie, who was very lively, did not fail, as he swallowed everything, to make facetious gibes about various people—but he spared the two Pharaohs and the high priest, whom he sensed were unassailable, and fell back on William, whose appetite and unquenchable thirst excited his envy.

"Say, Sir Shakespeare, I'd like to play, Hamlet. What do you think?"

"If you like," said William, phlegmatically. "I believe you're capable of any drollery. But if you do, change your name; it might not suit Charlie."

"Why?" said the little man, a great comedian of world cinema. Briskly taking off his moustache and wing, he suddenly displayed a pale and distinguished face, and pronounced in an astonishing fashion: "To be or not to be, that is the question..."

"Bravo! Hurrah! He's Hamlet in person. Hip, hip, hurrah for Charlie!"

"Well, Mr. Chaplin, when you play Hamlet, I'll play Falstaff. It's the only role I can play."

"Mr. Shakespeare," asked Countess Olivani-Sforza, "are you a descendant of the immortal poet?"

"I might have that glory, but I must confess that I have no idea. I know of no ancestors before my grandfather, a tavern-keeper in Yorkshire."

"The greatest glory is to be one's own ancestor," said Elphi Mordant, the iron king.

"And it's better to be Elphi Mordant than the King of Prussia, Emperor of Germany, Wilhelm II," said Charlie Chaplin. "One never ceases to rise, while the other has fallen."

Mordant made an amicable gesture to Charlie, who understood that he had just made a friend of the billionaire.

Diana, meanwhile, had set her role as the Pharaoh's wife somewhat to one side, in order to take on that of mistress of the house, and she was paying attention to her guests, addressing an amiable word to each of them. Ormus and Adsum had more difficult roles to play, but, by virtue of wit and poise, they avoided the slightly fantastic aspect of their situations. The ladies were a great help, interrogating them on mystical subjects, and the supper ended with general delight. Going with the flow, the billionaires forgot the Duke of Rutland and treated Ormus as the king of the fête.

They left the tables.

The orchestra struck up foxtrots, fashionable jazz-tunes, and other slightly drunken and profligate dance music.

Edison, who was among the guests, gazed at the immense glass edifice that had transformed the lawn into a hothouse in the middle of winter, sheltering palm-trees, laurier-roses and an entire lightly-dressed crowd. Addressing Dr. Adsum, with whom he had felt an immediate sympathy—Edison, the inventor of electric lighting, was costumed as Osiris, the defunct god who had represented Helios in ancient Egypt—he said: "Perhaps the day will come, when the terrestrial globe, chilled by the freezing of the sun, is in its death-throes, when humans will be obliged, in order to prolong their existence, to surround the Earth with an envelope capable of isolating it from the glacial ether, and replace the heat of the paternal star by means of electricity or some other artificial means. They will be forced to utilize, to that end, their resources of coal, naphtha and oil—which are, in sum. merely solar heat stored in cellars."

"Limited combustibles, Master."

"There is still the sea-bed, unexploited until now; it's merely a matter of finding the means to render it productive."

"What would you gain by that?" said Adsum. "In any case, the end of the world won't be caused by cooling. I've made observations personally over a hundred anterior centuries, and in that lapse of time the temperature has scarcely varied. That's not the danger for the people who will exist in millions of centuries. Moreover, in that era, the human race will have evolved and humans then will scarcely resemble those of today."

"You believe, Adsum, in a progression of human intelligence?"

"Certainly. You're the proof of it, as are we both. What do Edison and Adsum have in common with the cave-dweller I was fifteen thousand years ago?"

Edison was leaning toward the old mage, because the aged inventor was as deaf as a centenarian oak. "You've been able to go back that far? I'd like to have the same gift."

"You could, Mr. Edison, but it would be necessary for you to modify your way of working."

"Really? And you, Adsum—could you do what I do?"

"No. One human brain can't contain everything. I've only had three scientific incarnations, but you, Mr. Edison, have had four."

"Really? You're exciting my curiosity. That you can recover your own preceding incarnations is already a great marvel, but to know those of others..."

"I recognize those with whom I have previously lived."

"We're old friends, then?" said Edison, laughing.

"Great intelligences are rare. While I've pursued the psychic sciences, you have always studied the positive sciences. You were once Eratosthenes, the Alexandrian philosopher who let himself die of hunger at eighty, Diaphantus, the inventor of algebra, Herschel, the great astronomer and Christian Arsted, the physicist.[17] You can see that our acquaintance goes back a long way."

"My God! I need to research these individuals, to find out whether I can recover anything of my present character in those preceding incarnations."

They bumped into two men who had nothing Egyptian about them: William Shakespeare and Charlie Chaplin, both of them unsteady on their feet, moving with a drunken gravity.

"Ho! The high priest!" cried William. "Quickly, touch wood and iron!"

"Greetings, Mage!" said Charlie. "I'm waiting for your god to rise in order to go to bed."

"Listen, Adsum, to the words of a sage," said Shakespeare, "and profit from them. There is a tide in the affairs of men, which, taken at the flood, leads to fortune! Let it go, and it will never come again."

---

[17] Eratosthenes of Cyrene, who lived in the second century B.C., was not Alexandrian, although Diaphantus, the "father of algebra," who lived in the third century A.D., was. William Herschel (1738-1822) died before Edison was born in 1847 but the other name cited is very puzzling, given that there does not seem to have been time for another significant incarnation between Herschel's death and Edison's birth. I have rendered the name as the French text does, but there never was a physicist of that name; it looks like a misrendering of the name of the Danish physicist Christian Ørsted, or Oersted, but that would make no sense, as his dates (1777-1851) overlapped both Herschel's and Edison's.

"You're right, Master William—but don't worry about me; I'm a good pilot."

Charlie had taken off his little hat, which he was turning over in every direction.

"What do you hope to find in there, Mr. Chaplin?" Shakespeare asked him. "Your brain?"

Charlie, returning to his obsession, replied, as he contemplated his undersized headgear: "No, the thoughts of Hamlet, whose role I want to play. This, Sir, is not a hat but your skull. Poor Yorick! I knew him! He was a fellow of infinite jest, of most excellent fancy."

"Like you, Charlie."

"Shut up, Shakespeare, and take back your skull"— he exchanged hats with him—"or rather, that of your ancestor, the man you ought to be but aren't. O Shakespeare, are you or are you not?"

"I thirst—therefore, I am!"

"Let's drink, then, William. You can see that I'm drunk, but you can't see that I'm thirsty."

The two fantasists drew away. Then Edison and Adsum saw that Charlie had hung a gigantic gilded cardboard question mark on Shakespeare's back, and as they went away, he tapped William's back with his cane, repeating: "To be or not to be, that is the question..."

Edison, being hard of hearing and not up to date with literary matters, asked the bearded Mage in the white robe what the significance of Charlie's clowning was.

"A humorous allusion," replied the high priest of Helios. "Erudite people claim that Roger Manners, Earl of Rutland, was the true author of Shakespeare's works, and Charlie is amusing himself on that drunkard's back."

"And what do you think about that erudite confusion, my dear Master?"

"That the English nobility would be glad to pass off the work of the plebeian Shakespeare as the work of a gentleman."

"True glories always emerge from the people," said Thomas Edison.

XVI. The Day After the Fête

Daybreak, that cruel enemy of masquerades, had brought an end to the antique splendors. Beneath the rays of the rising sun, the panoramas and the simulated colonnades lost much of their grandiose aspect. Automobiles had carried away the guests, who, on emerging from the pomp of an Egyptian fête, encountered the glacial temperature of a December day outside.

One man, however, was still wandering in the hothouse, all alone, like Hamlet in the cemetery of Elsinore. William Shakespeare, after having put his new friend, Charlie Chaplin, in his Ford, and still a trifle drunk, was indulging in a monologue amid the deserted Egyptian setting. In Redge House, everyone was still asleep.

"How fortunes change! Yesterday, master of the house, today, I think my friend George is swinging in the wind. That's not what worries me—the Duchess will be generous—but I was like a pet cat here, attached to the household..."

"Mr. Shakespeare!" called the fresh and clear voice of a young woman.

"Over here, Ketty. Over here! What do you want, my blonde cherub? Do you need a bed-companion!"

"Get away, Mr. William! What do you take me for?"

"If I take you, charming Ketty, it will surely be for myself."

"Hark at you, the gallant beau! More apt to kiss a bottle than a girl."

"The former prepares for the latter, my beauty. A water-drinker is a paltry lover!"

"I've been looking for you for half an hour."

"It's the first time that a fair maiden has ever been so persistent. Well, here I am, entirely ready to oblige you."

"It's not on my own account. Milady wants to talk to you."

"I'll follow you—or rather, let's go together." And the gallant fellow put his arm around the maidservant's waist, and stole a kiss on the back of the neck.

"I'll forgive you, because you're a bit cracked."

"Lovers and madmen, my beauty, have seething brains. Like poets, they're full of imagination, and that imagination creates an artificial world."

"What's that supposed to mean?"

"That I think you're more beautiful and more inebriating than Venus."

"Personally, having less wit, I see you as Silenus."

Bantering thus, they had gone into the house, and Ketty, the dainty blonde, introduced stout William into the Duchess's apartment.

Clad in a delightful dressing-gown, the Duchess was stretched out on a divan. Exhausted by the fatigue of the night, Diana had not been able to close her eyes. So, having decided to put an end to her irresolution, she had sent for Shakespeare, as the worthiest intermediary between her and her husband. Ormus' kiss had chased away all hesitation. To continue playing a hypocritical role beside a man she despised, in order to live a life of worldly dissimulation, was too rude a task for the proud American woman. The welcome given to Fodor by her compatriots had made her understand that in their eyes, the Mage, adventurer as he was, counted as one of them. He was the conqueror of a fortune—by an original means, but all was fair in business.

Why hide, then? Was not the daughter of Nathan Bering, by virtue of her billions, above all convention? Did she not have every right? She had paid dearly for the title of Duchess and she would keep it, but she would dispense in future with a worldly constraint that lowered her in her own estimation.

"You must have slept very well, Master William, if it took you so long to answer my summons?"

"Far from it, Milady. I haven't closed my eyes. I was walking in a melancholy fashion, regretting that every feast comes to an end, and that it's necessary for us to resume the roles assigned by destiny."

"Are you speaking for yourself? Are you not, today as yesterday, William Shakespeare?"

"Which is to say, the shadow, the burlesque phantom of a great man."

"There are many who are even less. But I haven't brought you here to philosophize. It's as the Duke of Rutland's intimate friend that I want to speak to you, because I think you're the person best placed to get him to submit to my wishes, with suitable arrangements, in order not to offend his dignity."

"I anticipate what you're going to say, Milady—it's a matter of a separation."

"You said it. You saw what happened last night. Well, I love the Mage Ormus. A clandestine liaison is not for a woman like me. I'm taking back my liberty, no more and no less; the Duke will do the same, and that will be that. I thought at first about divorce, but in that case, the Duke would be left in poverty. An amicable separation will permit me to give him a pension. What do you think of five hundred dollars a month?"

"Is it as a representative of the Duke that I'm to consider that offer?"

"Certainly, for I know that he'll ask your advice."

"Then round out the sum, Milady. Say two thousand dollars, or twenty-five thousand a year, and George will be able to maintain his status."

"All right—and I'll throw in a thousand dollars a quarter for pocket-money for a certain William Shakespeare, so long as he stays with his friend. That, my dear William, is because I know that, although debauched, you're an intelligent man, and that so long as you're the Duke's mentor, he won't fall into base degradation."

"You flatter me, Milady. Be certain that, for as long as George wishes it, I'll be his most devoted friend. Similarly, I dare to say humbly that I'm yours."

"Thank you. By what I've just said to you, I've proved my esteem for you—so go and fulfill your mission. I hope that you'll do so honorably."

William kissed the Duchess's hand and went back to the Duke of Rutland's apartment.

The aristocrat had just woken up, his head heavy and his mouth wooden. He made an effort to recall the events of the previous evening, the Egyptian fête, and his wife in Ormus' arms. The memory was a trifle vague. On seeing William come in, the Duke, who had a bad headache, recalled that Shakespeare had been with him when he had surprised his wife.

"Damn!" he said. "You've arrived just in time. You can tell me whether or not I was dreaming."

"You weren't dreaming. If you're not a cuckold, it won't be long. Old chap, you see me in the role of ambassador."

"I can guess from whom."

"The Duchess thought that the blow might be less hard coming from me."

"How much is she offering?"

"Twenty-five thousand dollars a year. With that, one can show one's face in London or Paris."

"Then we're resuming the life of old, my old Will? Damned if I'll miss the United States. Do you recall our last year in Paris?"

"Yes—life was becoming difficult."

The two friends remembered the existence they had once led, when the Duke had almost reached the end of his resources, when usurers counting on his name and title had made him sign for loans at a hundred per cent interest. Finally, Aaron Lermmerfeld had unearthed him a rich heiress: Diana Bering, whose father, in his vanity as a billionaire, had bought her a noble title, as he might have bought her a string of pearls or a diamond necklace. The Duke had been forty then, with a physique as dilapidated as his fortune. Diana had only been nineteen, but, accustomed to giving orders and satisfying all her whims, she had acquired a natural authority that the Duke had never attempted to challenge.

Provided that he had social status and money in his pocket, he had left her absolute free to do exactly as she wished. In that fashion he had traveled the world, taking the inseparable Shakespeare with him. The latter's wit and whimsy allowed him to tolerate the Duke, who, without being a fool, was somewhat lacking in a sense of humor and spontaneity.

The Duke's allusion to his bachelor life reminded William of those days, long forgotten, but which had also been days of youth and facile pleasures. This time, they could see Europe again without the inconveniences of old, and live, in total freedom, the costly lives of those favored by fortune.

"Where shall we go?" Shakespeare asked.

"The season recommends the Côte d'Azur in France, or Biarritz. Has the Duchess fixed the day of departure?"

"No, but the sooner the better, I think. A Fabre Line steamer is leaving tomorrow."

"Well then, we leave tomorrow! Oh, my poor old chap, I was scared that she might want a divorce."

"There's no danger of that. Your wife paid dearly for the title of Duchess, and she'll hand on to it. When her infatuation for the Mage has deflated, she'll be quite glad to be the Duchess, as before. She's very keen to be Pharaoh's wife, but she knows that the title isn't in the Gotha."

"You don't think the adventurer will try to marry her?"

"I don't think so. Alongside the Mage there's the illuminatus Adsum. He won't let Ormus get his hands on the fortune alone. Then again, there's something of a Calvin or a Loyola in that old codger, and I don't believe he's ruthless or hypocritical."

"In sum, we have estimable adversaries. I like their doctrines; it's a pity that..."

"Their chief has made you a cuckold. Confess that he's very handsome and well placed to flatter the imagination with his charlatanry."

"Love doesn't see with the eyes, but with the imagination. That's why the god Cupid is represented as blind. Love doesn't always have good taste or judgment. Wings, but not eyes! That's the emblem of its scatter-brained vanity. And it's said that love is a child, because it's so often mistaken in its choice that it perjures itself all over the place."

"Bravo, George! Cuckoldry has given you philosophical ideas. Let's be glad, then, that we won't grow old in dry America."

XVII. Departed, Cuckolded and Content

Diana ostentatiously accompanied the Duke of Rutland and his rather solid shadow, the inseparable Shakespeare, aboard the transatlantic liner. So far as everyone else was concerned, the Duke was leaving for Europe to attend to a matter of succession. Thus, appearances—which are sufficient for society—were saved, and the separation could be final. For the billionaires of Fifth Avenue and Long Island, all those who had been present at the great Egyptian fête, there was no doubt as to the truth, but they knew Diana well enough not to spread any slander, and they all accepted a convention invoked without shocking anyone.

On returning to Redge House, Diana immediately went to see the two thaumaturges.

Without really being conscious of it, she hoped to find the Mage Ormus alone, and to resume the conversation interrupted by her husband's untimely arrival. Ormus' kiss had awakened a desire in the Duchess entirely other than that of studying psychic phenomena. At Diana's age, a woman in the plenitude of her vitality; there is a recrudescence of sensuality within her; mysticism, which is often no more than unslaked desire, gives way to amour, all the more violently if there is no reason to restrain it.

Ormus had told Adsum what had happened between Diana and himself, and that had occasioned a long discussion between them. The old man would have preferred to have an entirely chaste adept in the Duchess, a spirit as pure as himself and as he had hoped that Ormus would be, but his disciple, while understanding that carnal pleasure was a distraction from his goal, felt passions rising within him that he had only resisted previously by virtue of his desire to raise himself to his master's level by a complete renunciation of material satisfaction.

Adsum knew from his own experience how difficult it is for a man in the fullness of his strength to resist natural laws. In his youth, he too had made sacrifices to pleasure; but the love of science had taken precedence over the science of love, and he had wrought a voluntary devastation upon himself that put him beyond temptation. He had not dared to propose a similar method to Fodor, but he had achieved a similar result by an authoritative suggestion that had dampened the ardor of the young man's blood.

As for the Duchess, it was probable that the woman would carry away the neophyte, dragging along his pupil, disciple and prophet.

After mature deliberation, Adsum had decided that it was necessary to resist for as long as possible, in order to avoid a setback. Ormus, dominated by the old priest's will, had agreed with that opinion.

That subordination of a young and vigorous man might seem extraordinary, but Antal Fodor had spent his youth in India, in the company of Yogis, whose rule is absolute chastity; their principal aim is to separate the spirit from its carnal envelope in order to raise it above itself by meditation, and even to detach it altogether. Ormus, without having arrived at a result as complete as that, nevertheless practiced an austere regime, not allowing himself to be dominated by temporary sensation. For him, the Duchess was to be a necessary lever, and, once the obstacle was overcome, a useful instrument. As incapable of hatred as of love, he might give in to a physical weakness, but, as for all great ambitions, his dream was above carnal passions.

Adsum, naturally, sustained him on that path.

The Duchess was, therefore, rather excited when she went into studio of the two psychologists. At the sight of Adsum, she could not suppress an impulse of annoyance. The Mage did not appear to notice it.

"Well, my Daughter?" he asked.

"My uncertain spouse is now sailing for Europe. We're therefore free to devote ourselves to science without any worldly preoccupations. Aren't you tired, my Father, after the party? It's left me with nothing but disillusionment."

"My Daughter, nothing in life is worth the trouble of regret, any more than anything is worth the trouble of desire. If you want to be one of us, you must detach your spirit from everything material. I know that the human beast is avoid for brief pleasures, the idea of which haunts you, but reflect, my child of election, on their futility.

"These passions, which humans poeticize in order to ennoble them in their own eyes, are, in reality, merely a need imposed by nature for the preservation of the species. Look at other beings. What we have idealized is, for them, merely a rapid act having no more importance than drinking or eating. Humans, superior by virtue of speech, have sought to prolong the pleasure of the senses by any and every means, but they surpass the objective imposed by natural law; it leads to organic disorders that injure the psychic faculties. My hope, my dear Daughter, has been to raise you above humankind by combining your soul with ours, and thus creating a psychic trinity."

Under the influence of his authoritative gaze, Diana felt her resistance melting away; she was no more than soft wax ready to submit to the imprint of those two superior wills.

"My Father," she replied, "I am your most humble servant. Instruct me. Guide me."

"Give me your hands, both of you," said Adsum, "and let us link our souls likewise, in order that the magnetic fluid that streams through the worlds might be concentrated in us to elevate our spirit."

And, still under the influence of the authoritative gaze, Diana closed her eyes. The two men did likewise.

A religious silence reigned for a long time in the chamber of stars.

Anyone who had seen that singular scene would have wondered what the three individuals, seemingly petrified in an extraordinary cerebral tension, could possibly be doing.

XVIII. Spiritual Incantation

The old man spoke, in the profound silence of the young couple and the stars.

"Let us rise! Let us rise up perpetually! Beneath us, see the Earth hollow out like a cup, while the horizon grows and seems to descend below us. Let the laws of matter disappear! We, imponderable fluid, are no longer bound by them! What is gravity to those who no longer have weight? Heat to those who no longer have surface? Attraction to those who no longer have mass? Light to those who see without eyes and hear without ears? Watch the Earth, where so many people act, and because they have movement think that they exist, flees from us. Life is nothing if it is not ruled by spirit! See around us, shining in their millions, not a planet like the little ball we have just quit, but suns like the one that illuminates and vivifies the Earth. Look! Listen! Sense around us, among those monstrous globes, the universal palpitation of the soul of worlds.

"Look mystery in the face. A formidable wave circles through the Universe, animating all those heavenly bodies where beings live that are beyond or comprehension, humanities different from our own; heavenly bodies fecundated by a strange and flamboyant sap, flying through space from sun to sun. Comets, sources of planetary life, mysterious messengers of universal seed, plunge through limitless space, bearing immortal fecundity. My Daughter and my Son, let us draw closer to our Father who reigns in the heavens, the Sun. We have fled terrestrial influence. That is not enough; now we need to escape universal influence.

"It is necessary for us to know the *why* of what *is*. We witness transformations: matter, which is merely the present aspect of defunct life, renews that aspect incessantly and relentlessly; the molecules that compose our brains have existed in the prehistoric plesiosaur and mammoth. Everything, without pause, disappears only to be reborn. Only spirit endures, susceptible to progress. On the Earth, we have not yet evolved sufficiently to understand everything, but in many of these worlds circling in space, there are certainly civilizations more advanced.

"Into the azure! Forwards! If we Terrans can achieve the cerebral summation sufficient to subsist fluidically, we can escape to go in search of superior humankinds and acquire the knowledge that is still lacking down here."

Diana, her head reeling fearfully in the blue décor full of stars that surrounded her, representing the Immensity to her, yielded to the domination of the two mages. Each of them holding one of her hands, Adsum continued to hold her in the vertiginous precipices of thought.

"Don't be afraid, dear spirit, stay with us! That vast Universe is nothing; it is no more, in its amplitude, than the body of any being composed of atoms. If one were to throw into space all the grains of sand and drops of water on Earth, that dust would be less than all the worlds that surround us. Numbers lose all value here, since it is the incommensurable. The human mind demands a limit, for it wants a limit to everything, but here, there cannot be one. It is as impossible to imagine a limit to infinity as it is to imagine infinity. Infinity is a terrible word that

118

weighs upon the mind but tells us nothing. Nothing is finite in nature, since everything recommences.

"Is it not the same in this limitless milieu? Has it a center, a Universal navel, from which a will departs? We humans have acquired the habit of considering our Sun as the nucleus of life; it is merely the center of a planetary system, itself describing a mighty orbit around an unknown capital. Is that the universal point of departure of worlds? No! For our Sun is merely one star in the Milky Way, in which there are millions of suns. It is a splendid chaos, ordered of its own accord, with laws of attraction and the gravity of bodies acting upon one another.

"And that formidable amalgam of worlds and sun, we find once again in the most infinitesimal of beings. That animalcule, only visible in a microscope, is composed of millions of atoms, as the Universe is of millions of stars. Every atom has its individual life, dying and living again incessantly, perhaps progressively. We ought to accord a directing spirit to all organisms that reproduce. There is a spirit in the atom, since it exists, lives, dies and modifies itself. Is there, in that scale of beings, a primordial molecule, the basis of everything that exists? Humans have created words—cells, molecules—that signify no more than the word infinity. The almost-nothing, no matter how microscopic it might be, is a base of creation. Everything is divisible in the extreme, and when we want to take census of atoms, we count them in billions per square millimeter—which is a figure that surpasses our intellect.

"And the atom *is ourselves*; we are composed of that impalpable dust; it is us, and we are not, in sum, its masters. Those infinitely small entities regulate what, for them, is a universe; they impose their will upon it, make

119

it suffer, kill it, without it being able to do anything against them, since destroying them would be destroying itself. Well, why refuse those atoms, which compose everything that exist, a directing spirit of which we are the proof? Thus, molecular infinity exists as well as stellar infinity, and the infinitely small mirrors the infinitely large. Everything fuses and mingles, atoms and suns.

"And in addition to matter, the visible component of worlds, there is force, the fluids that we only know in part, as yet, and which are innumerable. These fluids include those that relate to animal and plant life, which are the intellectual parts of everything that exist. In the middle, if there is one, of that mysterious gulf of nature, the human mind, which is a supreme fluid in respect of it, struggles and seeks to understand. Ought we to renounce that and be content to live the beautiful life of the fortunate of the Earth, without that higher preoccupation? Or rather, should we lose our reason therein, go in search of the unknown, the incomprehensible, the great why?"

Adsum's thought, which was perceptibly communicated to the other two, Ormus and Diana, by his voice and his quivering fingers, paused.

The two dreamers seemed to wake up with a start among the stars, each with one hand under the empery of the hands of the Master Adsum, who was looking at them, as if his forehead were illuminated by an internal fire.

XIX. The Enchantment of Billions

That flight outside life had exhausted Dina mentally and physically. For Ormus, the sensation was not new; he knew that the domination of his mind was due to Adsum's spiritual supremacy over him, just as his own mind was the master of the Duchess. Now, that suggestion of a master thought, which fused the three minds into one, that voyage in infinity had become a reality for the Duchess; the two men had converted her physical awakening and the appeal of her senses into a sort of mental sensuality, an ecstasy of psychic love in the ether, a double friction and erosion of ideas, in an ideal orgy, to such an extent that the woman was exhausted by it. It seemed that her brain was stunned, sunk in a vague torpor.

Such moments are rare in the human species. Scarcely having fallen asleep, the mind travels anew, sometimes creating a veritable existence for us alongside the other, where the minutes count as hours. At other times, our brain gives birth to a kind of kaleidoscope, where events and beings mingle in a host of various impressions devoid of order and cohesion. Are dreams a kind of relaxation, or repose? It is permissible to doubt it, for some have a complication and an order more elevated than that of waking life, in which the mind— domesticated, so to speak—devotes itself to a more regular and less fantastic labor.

Adsum left the exhausted Duchess in that state of mental morbidity for a moment; then he extended the palm of his right hand over her, holding the fingers and thumb together, extended and imperious, in order to pour a dose of energy into her and revive her vacillating spirit.

She straightened up and smiled at the two mages.

"O Father" she stammered, "Are you a god?"

"The human imagination has created gods in order to focus adoration by lending them a form, a personality in its own image, and has given them names. But God, if there is a God, is incomprehensible. The human masses demand a god less vague, and our duty, as pastors of that immense flock, is to impose a divinity upon them that at least has a plausible rationale in his religion. Thus, the Ancients recognized as a primordial divinity the Sun, the father and fecundator of the Earth, to which he distributes light and hat: the Sun, the principal fire, with his twelve divisibilities, which are the signs of the zodiac and from which mythologies have taken divinities concordant with the months and the seasons: the twelve gods of Olympus, Hercules and his twelve labors, Jesus and his twelve disciples.

"In sum, I want to reestablish the true religion deformed by people and the centuries by a mixture of myths and schisms; a purified religion that returns to the source from which everything issues, more or less—the eternal Father, the Sun; to the veneration of a unique, visible and nurturing god.

"The Flower of Truth, founded on that natural and luminous base, abolishes eternal punishments, with are not only sins against bounty but against justice. The wicked are punished by themselves, because wickedness, which is a lack of wisdom, retards their psychic progress, stagnates them in inferior reincarnations, while the mentality of the sage rises ever higher.

"Here, in broad outline, is our new religion, established very simply, without obscure, prolix and destructive theologies:

"There is but one god who reigns in the heavens, the Sun, the principle of life and beauty.

"No salaried clergy, no temples, no icons. It only requires a propaganda by way of the press, regulated by a committee of sages elected by everyone, maintained by voluntary offerings whose surplus will be directed into scientific works.

"Fraternal aid between all humans, regardless of nationality; they are human, and that is sufficient.

"It is necessary not to kill that which bleeds, nor suppress that which vegetates. The plant that is uprooted and the tree that is cuts down must suffer as much as the fish one hooks or the kid whose throat is cut. Doubtless it is a law of life; humans, born to be both carnivorous and herbivorous, as their jaws prove, cannot spare plants and animals, but ought to make them die only in accordance with their needs, with as little cruelty as possible.

"Time and distance have no real value except in the human mind, and in the context of universal life, do not exist. Intelligence exists in everything, feeblest in the atom and the mite, at its apogee in human beings, but superior, doubtless formidable in the heavenly bodies and our sun, which are the supreme progress of the atom and are the true faces of god.

"That is our gospel. We shall analyze it and develop it without further delay, rendering it accessible to any intelligence; and henceforth, my Daughter, it is to the three of us, its founders, who are responsible for that work."

Adsum fell silent.

Diana's brain was seething under the influence of these ideas, new to her. Previously, like all Anglo-Saxons, she had—without any genuine faith, it is true—practiced the Bible, which, in her eyes, was the book of revelation that no other could replace. It seemed paltry now, that incongruous ensemble of parables, debatable in its morality, corresponding as well as could be expected to the history of a nomadic people: a population of shepherds mutating into warriors and creating a god of wrath and pride, Jehovah. Henceforth, Diana Bering could strip away, overnight, her womanhood and the weakness of her sex, accentuated by the colossal fortune. After the vanity of her incarnations as Pharaoh's wife, Cleopatra and Empress Eudoxia, now she was being summoned to be the proselyte and prophetess of a religion destined to rule the Earth. One day, in centuries to come, she would be the equal of a Buddha, a Jesus or a Mohammed, lauded by posterity.

The two mages read what was passing through the American woman's mind as in a book, and knew that it meant certain success for the propaganda of their work—but they could not think without bitterness about the baseness of the means they had employed for the conquest of that magnificent prey.

"Everything I have belongs, from now on, to your great idea," she said, firmly. "There could not be any nobler goal for my unspeakable fortune, and the nobility of our work will redeem its origin and its immortality."

"To work, then!" said Ormus. "I'll go to New York to see Pytor and reach an understanding with him." He added: "Now that's settled, permit me to submit an idea to you that occurred to me three days ago, Diana, in the midst of that somewhat theatrical fête reconstituting the life that we lived together long ago: the idea of seeing in place a region, a country, the sight of which will doubtless recall a magnificent epoch of my anterior life—and also yours, since I was your spouse in those times. I find the idea tempting. Before leaving, we can issue directives setting down the broad outlines of our propaganda. Would you like, Diana, while all that is being organized, to undertake a voyage to Egypt?"

"What do you think, my Father?" asked the catechumen.

"I see no objection to it. The *Daily Mail* is already ringing the bells in a series of articles inspired by us; it will continue, and during the time in Egypt, the necessary arrangements can be made for lecture-tours, in New York, Philadelphia and San Francisco to begin with. After that, we'll see."

"We'll have to combat hundreds of sects and petty chapels. It will be difficult to supplant the Bible in the Union; it's deeply rooted there."

"We won't mount a frontal attack right away, and I think it would be wise to make use of skillfully-drawn cuttings. The Bible is a mess of old junk and absurdities, from which one can draw all kinds of deductions. We'll find some favorable texts therein."

"In that case," said Ormus, "I think we can head for Egypt in mid-January."

"And I'll make every effort," said Adsum, "to discover the real tomb of Tut-Ankh-Amun."

PART TWO: THE PHARAOH'S KISS

I. The Arrival in Egypt

As soon as they had passed through the Strait of Messina the travelers perceived a new world opening before them. The warm and perfumed atmosphere already reeked of the Orient. In the Liparian archipelago they went past the orange-gardens of Panarea and Stromboli. The dawn rose, blonde and gilded, over lapis-lazuli waves; violet spangles glittered on the waves, scarcely fringed by a fine lace of foam, while the snowy summit of volcano on the horizon—Etna—sparkled like a splendid diamond in the light of the rising sun.

On the ninth of January 1928, Diana set foot on Egyptian soil, with her two companions. Ten years previously, she had made that classic voyage in the company of the Duke of Rutland, and had conserved a rather disgusted memory of it. That journey through the cosmopolitan palaces, with so little relationship to Egyptian life, had not encouraged her to recommence it in the same conditions; finding Alexandria too worldly, she had preferred to disembark at Rosette.

Three automobiles had been loaded on to the largest of the billionairess's yachts, the *Pharaoh*—caravans of a sort, designed for speed and habitation—the first for the Duchess and her chambermaid, the second for Adsum and Ormus, and the third for the kitchen and the servants, three of whom were chauffeurs and one a cook. These motor-caravans were a masterpiece of comfort and luxury. Everyone, in accordance with their status, was comfortably accommodated, with the least possible embarrassment.

The disembarkation of the automobiles took some time. Ormus decided to hire a dahabieh to go up the Nile as far as Cairo. The yacht would go through the isthmus of Suez, and reach Djibouti via the Red Sea, where it would wait for the travelers.

Rosette—or Rachid, to give it its Arab name—was a cluster of tall houses of alternating black, red and yellow bricks, pleasantly aligned. The inhabitants having no taste for regularity or uniformity, the overall effect was a veritably fantastic confusion in which cement, brick and wood competed in polychromatic harmonies. Antal Fodor had telegraphed from there to Cairo to hire the dahabieh and the response was immediate; the *Ibis* would be in Rosette the following morning.

After a stroll in the town, they went back aboard the yacht for dinner.

"I like Rosette much more than Alexandria," said the Duchess, as she sat down at the table. "Here, one is truly on the threshold of the Orient, whereas in Alexandria, which is an inn for the world, one rubs shoulders with all races."

"And not typical," Adsum replied, "for the majority of those who visit Egypt are enfeebled or worn out cosmopolitans who retain no special characteristics."

"Is a fortune a cause of degeneration then, Master?"

"Yes. Furthermore, marriage between old aristocracies enfeebles their produce. Proof: the representatives of surviving monarchies are all rachitic or idiotic."

"It's a good thing for them, then, when decrepit aristocrats marry a daughter of an energetic race along with a fine dowry."

"Energy is rare nowadays. What is gained through sports is lost again through alcohol and narcotics— although it hardly matters that the physical strength of humans is diminishing; only the intelligence interests us. The health and strength of the body can only give impulsion to the mind, though. All three of us are healthy, handsome and sturdy, and our mentality is worthy of its envelope."

"Tell me, my Father, do you think we should stay in Cairo for a while?"

"Yes, for I haven't seen El Kaïra since the fifteenth century. I was then the caliph Ibn-Qualcum,[18] but I suppose nothing much remains of the work I accomplished in that epoch."

"Well, we'll stay there as long as you please. Tomorrow, the automobiles and the dahabieh will be at our disposal, and we can rent a domicile that suits us, for I'm averse to palaces. Can you imagine that ten years ago, instead of excursions, we spent an entire week at a tennis tournament in the grounds of the hotel where we were staying."

"That's how aimless people travel."

At that moment, John Maryatt, the captain of the yacht, came into the room. "The weather is superb. Would Madame the Duchess like to take advantage of it for a moonlight trip?"

"That's a good idea, Captain."

A quarter of an hour later, Diana, Adsum and Ormus took their places in a steam-launch. The sea was

---

[18] The only actual 15th century caliph of Cairo with a name remotely similar to this was Al-Qa'im, who accomplished nothing during his four-year rule.

smooth and transparent. The stars were reflected therein, giving the impression of traveling between two skies.

When they reached Abukir, few lights were shining on the shore. The large wooden cabins, fitted out as rustic lodgings, were only inhabited in summer; the village, which was quite extensive, had thus been deserted by its tenants. Only a few poor Arabs stayed there all year round. The casinos were also closed. Only one, near the airfield, cast the melancholy pallor of its lights over the Nile, along with the distant sounds of a mechanical piano. Beyond the low-lying town the Lakes of Edkou and, further away, Mariotis were visible.

II. In the Dahabieh

When they awoke the following morning, a bizarre song attracted the attention of the travelers: a nostalgic tune measured by the rhythm of the oars: "*Hey! Hey! Allah, oûa Mohammed rassoul Allah!*"—which meant "Courage, brothers, Mohammed is the elect of Allah."

It was the captain, the Reïs, of the dahabieh hired the previous evening, who was coming in a launch to receive his orders. John Maryatt greeted him, and while they waited for the passengers to get up, the two men walked up and down the deck smoking cigars.

The Reïs, a Nubian, was superb; about thirty, alert and well-built, he was a head taller than Maryatt. He was an independent captain, the owner of the dahabieh, the *Ibis*. His majestic bearing, his handsome face, his jet-black moustache and his immense eyes, like black diamonds, gave him the air of one of those fierce pirates of which Europe had so much trouble purging the Mediterranean. His lips were thick and sensuous, and his costume was embroidered with gold. He identified himself simply as Ahmed—and the rich foreigners who had hired the dahabieh were obliged to pay for its owner too.

When Ahmed was introduced to the Duchess and the two mages, he bowed respectfully and put himself under the American woman's orders, having divined immediately that she was the yacht's owner.

"You seem to me to be an experienced man," said Diana. "We plan to go up the Nile as far as Cairo, where our automobiles will be waiting for us, with which we shall explore the shores of the river. When the opportunity presents itself, we'll come aboard, whenever an interest calls upon us to cross from one bank to the other. As much as possible, you'll keep pace with us, at every stage, in order that we don't have to search for you. Is that all right?"

"Perfectly, Milady."

"Good! Reïs, you'll have lunch with us on the yacht, before we go to your vessel."

The travelers were soon aboard the dahabieh, the *Ibis*. The Egyptian dahabieh has varied very little since ancient times, save for those of European construction, which, with their iron hulls, are reminiscent of motor-boats. The *Ibis* had a wooden hull, and the interior con-sisted simply of a single large cabin whose ceiling was the deck. The two extremities of the boat, which were very high, were ornamented with figures and lotus-flowers that were quite well-carved. There were two masts planted at the two ends, supporting two enormous sails fixed on long, slightly curved yard-arms. Such sails are not furled, but can be lowered and folded up. The wind was good and warm, but ten boatmen could move the long and heavy vessel against a contrary wind, using oars or sculls.

The Delta is the most fertile region of Egypt; trees, fruits, flowers and cereals all grow there in splendid abundance. Between Alexandria and Cairo the Nile passes through a country that varies little but whose mo-notony is rich in colors and perfumes, of which one does not tire. In that feast for the eyes, five or six different kinds of acacias mark out the route; from time to time, alternating with cypress or Alep pines, clumps of al-mond-trees, orange-trees, lemon-trees, fig-trees and quince-trees fill the air with vehement scents. And above everything, a profusion of climbing roses flows over an-ything that gives them a point of support, embalming the atmosphere, adding a divine drunkenness to the inebriation of other essences.

Immense date-palms laden with enormous clusters of fruit, coconut-palms and bananas border the route. There are also carobs, the feast of the Arab nomad, *nahea*, with delicate fruits that taste like apples, and *gechtahs*, from which one obtains a delicious creamy fluid. Arab huts disseminated along the route, constructed of dried wood and camel-dung and painted in vivid colors—blue, yellow, orange, almost always surrounded by apricot-trees, add their picturesque realism to the calmly moving landscape.

Vast fields of cotton cover the open ground. On the road to Abukir an Arab leads a few camels attached in Indian file. Half way to Abukir, an automobile passes by rapidly, striping the charm of the Egyptian spring: a fire-red limousine coming from the palace of Montazah, where King Fuad I resides in summer.

A few water-buffalo are bathing in the Nile, and near the enormous beasts, a little naked Arab girl, like a supple and slender bronze statuette, is playing and paddling in the water.

The *Ibis* glides over the quivering waves unhurriedly, and the villages established on the shore everywhere that an elevation of the ground above the level of the annual flood permits file past the passengers' eyes: to the east, El Bazreh, Berinhat, and Matvabis; to the west, Mohallet, Edfinah, and Dai Proutsh—at which they make a halt.

A dragoman responsible for food supplies purchased supplies throughout the voyage. The dragoman, a Hindu named Mojah Singh, had joined the dahabieh at Berinhat. The Duchess having opened unlimited credit, Mojah paid no heed to expense and bought everything he could find of the highest quality. At Beïrout, linked by two broad canals to Lake Edkou, fishermen came to offer fish whose trumpet-shaped noses give them a comical appearance—uncommon fish brought in summer by the flood. Henri, the French cook, prepared them perfectly, according to Ahmed's instructions, and they were declared excellent.

As they were drinking the coffee, the sound of a frantic gallop was heard on the bank. An imperative voice shouted: "Where is the Reïs? Let him show himself."

Ahmed, who was smoking at the prow, turned his head and saw a perfectly-harnessed horseman. "What do you want?"

"To tell you to take someone aboard."

"Impossible! I have passengers."

"Beware of my courbache!" He cracked a long whip with leather thongs, a part of which was looped around his wrist.

The handsome Ahmed reddened with anger. He leapt ashore, armed with a cane, and ran at the man who had insulted and threatened him. The latter turned his horse and kept his distance.

"Hey there!" said another horseman, arriving at a gallop. "Put down your stick, fellow. I'll pay fifty piastres for my passage. I have business in Chindiyoum and need to cross the river, nothing more."

Attracted by the noise, Diana and her companions looked at the new rider through the window of the cabin. Save for a tarboosh, he was dressed in the European manner, very elegant in his appearance.

"If the gentleman only wants to cross the Nile," said Ormus, "it won't delay us much."

"Certainly," said Diana. "Go on, Reïs, take the traveler across; we'll take a turn around Beïrout while we wait."

The man in the tarboosh got down from his horse and threw the bridle to the Arab. "Go away," he said. Then, approaching the bank, he said: "If I'm not mistaken, it's Madame the Duchess of Rutland that I have the honor of greeting?"

"You know me?"

"I've only seen you once before, ten years ago in Constantinople, at the British embassy."

"I did indeed make a voyage to the Orient at that time, but..."

"You don't recognize me? I would be very proud if it were otherwise, but I could not forget a woman as beautiful as you."

The Duchess started laughing. "I haven't come to Egypt in search of compliments."

"In that case, Duchess, you must do what our women do and hide your face. And be sure that if important business did not oblige me to go to the other side of the river, I would be reluctant to take advantage of your kindness—but I'm awaited, you see." With his hand, he indicated a compact group on the opposite bank, which was growing progressively. Again he bowed and leapt into the dahabieh, which drew away rapidly, propelled by the ten oarsmen.

"I don't remember that gentleman at all. If he was at the embassy, he must be some pasha."

"Ah!" said the Mage Ormus, who had aimed his binoculars. "It seems to me that he's getting a warm welcome."

Half an hour later, the dahabieh returned. Ahmed seemed very embarrassed.

"You seem to be annoyed, Reïs," observed the Mage.

"With good reason! I've just lacked respect for my sovereign. That's Fuad I, the king of Egypt."[19]

"The descendent of the Pharaohs—of us!" said Ormus, smiling at Diana.

The journey up the Nile continued. The wind was slightly stronger, and they made more rapid progress.

"We'll be in Kafrez-Laiya by nightfall," said the Reïs. "Would you like to spend the night there, or would you prefer to go on? The wind is good; we could reach Cairo by tomorrow morning."

"Let's travel through the night, then," said Adsum. "We'll arrive at our destination sooner. This commencement of civilization doesn't interest me much. After the Egyptian sovereign, we'd be capable of encountering the true one—the British High Commissioner."

They passed another ten villages before reaching Kafrez-Laiya, the head of the railway line to Cairo. Beyond that town, the Nile and the Katatben Channel are bordered on the right by the Libyan desert. The landscape unfurls invariably, still as flourishing and spring-

---

[19] Fuad I (1868-1936) had previously been the Sultan of Egypt, but when the United Kingdom recognized Egypt's theoretical (but not yet practical) independence in 1922 he changed his title to King and introduced a new Constitution giving him enormous powers; that Constitution was still in force in 1928 although he was forced to withdraw it in 1935 and restore power to parliament. His appearance as a character in the novel—especially in view of the role he plays when he reappears on the scene—is a trifle surprising, but it is possible that Champsaur had met him long before in Paris, when both men were young, and felt entitled to exercise a certain familiarity.

like on one side; sand-dunes and hills on the other. The wind had dropped completely, and they were obliged to continue by means of the oars, so they did not see the high minarets of Cairo appear until rather late the next day.

III. Old Cairo

On seeing the automobiles, the Reïs, who, out of a curiosity that might have been tactical, had followed the travelers to the garage, could not retain an admiring exclamation. Turning to Ormus, whom he considered as the director of the expedition, he said: "I see, my lord, by the equipment of your vehicles, that you have the firm intention of avoiding the great palaces. I suspected as much from a few words overheard on the way: you like the Orient for its intimate charm and ancient beauty. I share your taste, being one of the last of my race not to be Europeanized. If you will permit, I can show you a Cairo that not many foreigners see. My presence aboard is not necessary; the dragoman can take the dahabieh as far as El-Medinet, where we'll catch up with it. What do you say to my proposal?"

"We accept, Reïs Ahmed," Diana replied.

"Would you care to make a sacrifice to modernism, then, and take a tram?"

"Yes," said the Duchess. "That would be most amusing."

They went to the Mehidah El Ismaïlis square, where they took the tram, which took them via the El-Khoubri and Abdul Aziz Boulevards to Atabet-El-Hadra square. Until then, there was no reason to believe that they were in Egypt except for a few scattered architectural pretensions in imitation of Muslim art.

Diana was delighted with the tram-ride; until then, in the course of her life as a billionairess, she had never boarded a public vehicle, and the promiscuity of the reduced-price travelers interested her.

Directly facing her was a local woman dressed in a black silk sebleh. Her white veil, gently retained by a circular copper headband, indicated a coquette. In the mass of fabrics, all that could be seen of the woman was her eyes, but they were admirable eyes, which looked alternately at the Mage Ormus and the magnificent Reïs, whose handsome face had not influenced the Duchess. Evidently, the beauty—for she could not be ugly with such eyes—was making comparisons, and her choice appeared to fall definitively on Ormus, whose golden eyes seemed to her to be topazes; she then adopted a manner of draping herself in her ample vestment that showed off all the harmony of what was underneath.

Diana congratulated his Mage jokingly in English on his success, but, to her annoyance, was interrupted by the indigene.

"Have no fear, Madame. I make statuettes in the manner of the ancient potters of Tanagra. If I observe your friend's eyes"—she emphasized the word *friend*—"it is solely as an artist. I do not make a habit of hiding my impressions and I admire beauty wherever I encounter it, is you as well as in these gentlemen."

Although Alexandria is a quasi-European city, Cairo has maintained, in spite of its trams, its broad avenues, electricity and the profusion of tourists and English soldiers, the undeniable cachet of a truly Oriental city. The exceedingly high sky does not always have the blue profundity that poets attribute to it, because of the breezes of Suez, the Nile barrage, and the Aswan irrigations, but all races and colors mingle there with a picturesque and variegated garishness. Extremes meet: alongside the agitation of the center there are profound silences. Avenues crackling with sunlight are in close proximity with somber and narrow side-streets, and that salad of squalor, luxury, civilization, antiquity, beauty and ugliness, the European and the Oriental, forms a fine exotic tableau.

"I don't know," the Reïs said, "what the future has in store for my country, but it's necessary to take it as it is. The English have the gift of transforming everything they touch in their own image. Once, we were unacquainted with rain; they built the barrage, and now it rains three or four times a year. Gradually, they are eating into the desert, converting it into palm plantations. I detest and admire those practical organizers. Cairo is becoming healthy; gardens are growing everywhere; circulation is easier, the roads better maintained.

"Personally, I have renounced the struggle against these raptors who want to conquer the world. Germany hinders them and competes with them, but they will be able to defeat Germany, making use of France, by appearing to come to its aid. One rival beaten, another surges forth—America. Against that one, not much can be done. The eater will be eaten. Imperialism, which has been able to conquer by virtue of the force of money and every hypocritical means with long teeth, will escape it, and its emancipates will deny the mother-land.

"England is like an overloaded vessel; it is low in the water and its hull is leaking. Will it sink to the bottom? A day will come when England, reduced to itself, will extend its hand to the other nations. On that day, it will not find a friend, and the people that it has lifted out of the rut will turn their backs on it, for it has taught everyone that selfishness in a law and a duty."

They had arrived at the Zuweila Gate, Byzantine in appearance, with its square bastions, its rounded vault, its covered passages and its two minarets.

"Nasr, the assassin of Caliph El Haïr," said the Reïs, "was captured by the Templars under that gate and delivered, for a large payment, to the women of the harem, who, after having tortured, mutilated and blinded him, sent him through the streets as far as here, the Bab al-Zuweila, in order to be nailed to it, alive. The vizier Dangam was decapitated there and thrown to the dogs for having had the audacity to take money from the mosques in order to pay his troops. Here too, Saladin had all the black troops who had dared to resist him executed, to the last man—and that extermination took two days. Here, again, the Mongol envoys were decapitated who had come to call on the city to surrender, and the mameluke Kutus then had the heads exposed on the wall. It required a great deal of blood, as you see, to make those two minarets sprout and grow."

Having got down from the tram, they were now walking through the city, and as they came into El-Naggar street they encountered a water-bearer. Once, the corporation was quite numerous, but today the city is sufficiently garnished with public drinking-fountains. Nevertheless, the Arabs of the old quarters continue to make use of the water-sellers, who carry it in a bladder equipped with a metal tube passed under the arm. It is doubtless the apparatus in question that gave the soldiers of the French army of Egypt the practical idea of the portable fountains of the old licorice-water merchants. The water-seller was holding a metal cup, which he offered to passers-by while intoning a kind of chant perhaps dating from the time of the Pharaohs.

"O you who are thirsty, come! Let him who cannot pay drink all the same. Come and drink, free of charge!"

The American woman thought that invitation so patriarchal and fraternal that she slipped a gold coin into the worthy man's hand. He was so impressed that he forgot to replace his stopper, and the liquid washed the feet of the passers-by, to the great joy of the street-urchins who were escorting the travelers, crying: "Baksheesh! Baksheesh!"

Passing from street to street they reach the square where the largest of the mosques, that of Sultan Hassan, is located. Then, going through an inextricable tangle of side-streets and cul-de-sacs, swarming with a dense population of workers, merchants, porters, donkey-drivers with thin animals and people with petty ambulant trades, they pass other mosques of dilapidated munificence. They stop for lunch.

Afterwards, on turning the corner of El Asrafiyeh, the principal street that continues El Nabayouyeh, they find the busiest quarter of Cairo in full activity. The cries of camel-drivers, street-vendors and donkey-drivers and the braying of donkeys overlap deafeningly.

A bus full of tourists, harassed by the merchants advanced with difficulty through the crowd, which does not get out of its way. The driver, in a blue robe and a small striped waistcoat, and the dragoman, make every effort to clear a path: "Look out! Clumsy fool!" The tourists, tired and bewildered, are somnolent in the heavy heat and the dust, for the kamsin is blowing from the desert and the air is saturated with impalpable sand, which penetrates everywhere.

Then there are the souks, where jewelers, wood-carvers and artists in metal work in the doorways of tiny boutiques. Here is the perfume bazaar, where, for twenty francs, one can get a minuscule bottle containing five or six drops of attar of roses. There is the spice-bazaar, and cinnamon, vanilla, clove, nutmeg and aloes assail passer-by violently, who are imbibing assorted aromas without opening their purses. Then there is the carpet-merchant, who invites you to visit his emporium. And all these bazaars are swarming with the robes of men and women. In the harsh light, on little carts loaded with watermelons, oranges, lemons and juicy pomegranates, everything shines with varied colors. Long skirts in olive-green, royal blue, garnet or striped silk fabrics come and go, jostling one another, surrounding tourists and interpreters, who are calling out to one another, and clapping their hands to summon coffee-sellers—who bring them an aromatic and perfumed essence in a tiny cup.

There are a great many bazaars, but the most curious is the one located near the Muhammad Ali mosque beside the citadel. There are gathered the merchants of gold and precious stones, and the engravers of copper plates. Marvelous hand-stitched kimonos imported from China or India swing on ropes. There is a heap of carpets in harmonious colors; prayer-rugs from Persia or Bukhara, as sickly as female tresses—in the times when women did not wear page-boy cuts that leaving the nape of the neck bare.

Here is the merchant of glazed fruit, who accosts you, makes you taste, and slips a packet into your pocket in spite of our protests. There are hundreds of them, coming and going, calm and smiling, never getting annoyed, so amiable, so polite, that one dare not hurt their feelings, and one buys in order to be agreeable to them. The indigenes, especially the women, go from one shop to another, sitting down on the brick benches in the boutiques, chatting for hours, nibbling a fruit, drinking a sherbet bought from an ambulant seller.

Thanks to the Reïs, the Duchess, Adsum and Ormus pass through that tumultuous crowd quite rapidly.

IV. A Parenthesis for Alexandria

Diana Bering, Duchess of Rutland, the Pharaoh's Wife, had neglected Alexandria in her itinerary, associating her memory of it with a honeymoon trip devoid of pleasure. That delightful city deserves better, however. In spite of the caprice of the characters, therefore, a quick sketch, the impression of the day of arrival:

In the pink and transparent shade, Alexandria is no more than a flat white line sparkling in the young morning sun. The quays come toward the gigantic transatlantic liner, and the sanitary service joins the police thereon. White uniforms, broad belts of red leather, scarlet tarbooshes mingle with the European or American passengers who watch the colors and the luminous magnificence of the movement, curious and astonished.

One is finally in Egypt, after the tedium of the severe and arrogant customs. After the docks, filled with yellow Arabs, the streets are swarming with robes, goats, donkeys and horses with turquoise collars. With a little squalor and a great deal of noise, all races and al colors of skin, all languages and all religions rub shoulders; there are Greeks in fustanellas; there are old Arabs with malicious wrinkled eyes, smoking their nargilehs at the doors of the indigenous cafés, daydreaming; there are young ones, in loose robes of white-striped cloth, or silk for the better-off, playing football, or fighting, howling like young wild animals.

"Arabia" files past, according to the indications the client gives, if he is capable of giving any, to the arbagui: "*Yalminack! Semalack! Doogri!*"—Left! Right! Straight ahead!

Here is the immense Ahdan bazaar, populated by Jewish and Muslim merchants. One can buy pistachio-nuts, cooked grains, biblidia, dates, and the local dried fruits. And, turning into an old street without sidewalks, full of debris, here is the sea again, the pretty "bahra," as blue as a sapphire, with a ruined fort profiled on the horizon.

Now there is the European quarter, elegant, chic, modern, too neat. A magnificent coast road that goes all the way to the king's palace, majestic and variegated, on the road to Abukir, serves as a promenade in the evenings. Under the burning midday sun, however, when everyone is taking a siesta, Arab children crouch down on the cool stones in the shade and, happy and tranquil, open their loose robes and search for their lice, like little apes.

On the Saïd Boulevard, the buildings, with large columns of pink marble, are radiant with light. In one of them is a café. It is not a banal place in which one hastens to conclude one's consumption because other clients are waiting for seats; it is a salon where people meet and watch pretty women go by in a harmonious décor. Large rooms, with rich woodwork, mosaics of gold and precious stones are furnished with comfortable bright armchairs. Palm trees and flowers are everywhere. Elegant, refined people savor a Turkish mocha served with a glass of iced water.

Outside, life swarms intensely. By way of the large and spacious Misjala street one reaches Fouad street. It is the wealthy quarter of the city, with sumptuous shops, mostly belonging to Syrians: the luxurious commercial center. The carriage trade is organized as in Paris, well-varnished and well-cared-for vehicles carrying rich foreigners or modern Muslims, perhaps to amorous rendez-vous.

At Groppi's patisserie, the upper crust of Alexandria gather at tea-time; people talk about the races, bridge, clothes and Paris—Paris! Ah, Paris!—feverishly, desirously, lovingly. To one side, in Fouad Street, so elegant, are two mosques and cinemas.

Beneath the ardent sun, flowers pullulate in the white and yellow city, inebriating it with the perfume of delicate roses; the city gives an impression of health, of happiness, of wealth, which one does not find elsewhere, even in Cairo. Everything is pretty or beautiful, everything is full of joy.

When dusk invades the immense bay that forms the harbor, the view is charming; along the coast road the casinos fill with laughter and cheerful music, with jazz. Above the marvelous villas, with their Edenic gardens, floats the sky, so blue and so pure: the African sky, calm and infinitely beautiful.

V. Cairo Again

Diana wanted to spend a second day in Cairo. Everything amused her, even the beggars—how numerous they are in Cairo!—demanding baksheesh, the merchants with their obsessive *"Sett! Sett! am el marouf!"* (Madame, I beg you), the little donkeys trotting lightly along and the little shoe-shiners.

So many tourists, foreigners, automobiles and electric trams in the broad avenues! So many large stores and dance-halls! A rich fellah goes by, paunchy beneath his robe of embroidered silk, his eternal amber chaplet between his ring-laden fingers. He resuscitates, among these modernities, the magic of the Orient.

Old Coptic churches and incongruous bazaars that reek of incense neighbor patissiers baking their pastries in the open; indigenous children feast on khishnah—sugared vermicelli—or loukomades, a kind of frothy Armenian fritter. Little pistachio-merchants harass you: *"Smchi!"* (Go away!) you cry, but the wretched child persists, begging, and you give him a piastre, which he takes while capering like a goat and which he gives to the patissier: *"Cailakierach, sett!"* (Many thanks, Madame.)

And on the large indigenous houses, the mashrabiyas of dark wood, behind which young Muslim women are looking out on the street, watching the Europeans—mysterious cages in which little feminine souls are perhaps getting bored. But no! They know nothing of liberty, dreams, the desire for space; they know nothing, those young Muslim women of old Cairo, of theaters, cinema or dancing; they have never heard the enervating, tender and puerile love-songs of handsome young men; they are unaware; they are happy behind their brown shutters, amused and astonished that these Europeans should come from so far away, even from Paris, to see houses like theirs, and old and arrogant Bedouins.

The entire city extends before you with its centuries-old minarets; the almost immense city with its white houses, its sunlit terraces, its marvelous gardens, its mosques, its bazaars, its souks, its cosmopolitan palaces, a mixture of charming exoticism and brash modernism: Cairo, the ancient city where all races mingle, where the ardent desert wind passes through, which sometimes causes the burning gilded sands to dance before the eyes.

Then, there is the descent toward the present Cairo, animated and joyful, with tourists dressed in bright hues, and always the dirty and ragged little beggars swarming around the Ezbekieh, a splendid garden of rare species and harmonious colors. Around it are the great avenues bordered by palm-trees, where the most beautiful residences are, and the palace of the ex-Khedive.

After the Qasr al-Nil bridge, another center, this one commercial. All the shops are crowded here, bright and cheerful in the benevolent and cool shade. At the fashionable patisserie and elegant and perfumed crowd gathers on Sunday mornings and the garden of Groppi's then resembles a vast flower-basket.

At the Zoo, one of the most beautiful in the worlds, shady and perfumed with delicate flowers, pink ibises stroll at liberty on the pale green lawns, beside a pool where nenuphar lilies grow, and all sorts of animals, even very rare ones, are amusing to behold.

Night-clubs and dancing-halls pullulate, bearing Parisian names like *Le Perroquet*. In the midst of the heat, softened by the warm breeze scented by inebriating flowers, all those Levantines, Europeans and rich indigenes ruminate their desire for that Paris. Blasé individuals avid for illusion sit down at table before an iced whisky and watch music-hall artistes singing to the strains of a negro orchestra. They search for memories of Paris, or are nostalgic for a Paris they have not yet seen.

And the Syrian women with bronzed velvet eyes and long curly lashes, the European women in silk dresses and ermine hoods, the men in smoking-jackets, are all thinking, as they go back along the spacious streets that overlook the *gafu*—the night-garden—about the same thing: Paris; without savoring the poetry of the city of mosques, without perceiving the beauty of the Oriental night, of Leilah, full of sweetness and perfumes.

On the stage, a blonde with a pale face starred with two blue eyes, of which there are none in Cairo, a graceful, mischievous gamine clad in silk chiffon, with no other jewelry than her youth—a blonde from Paris—sings: "Paris, king of the world..."

The Duchess, Adsum and Ormus are among the audience, and Diana is astonished to see he two mages amusing themselves frankly, abandoning their habitual gravity to applaud the young woman.

"My Father," she says, timidly, to Adsum, who is busy making his glass of champagne froth by stirring it with a cocktail-stick, "how is it that you're enjoying yourself in this environment?"

"Do you take me for a supernatural being, my Daughter? I was born of a woman, like all men, and my father, in Norway, was merely a humble timber merchant. Christ himself was born of a carpenter. The spirit, like the body, needs rest. One cannot always soar, without folding one's wings from time to time."

Ormus, as a sign of approval, intones softly: "Paris, king of the world…"

VI. The Pyramids

Renouncing a further prolongation of their stay in
Cairo, the Duchess and her companions decided to make
a classic visit to the pyramids of Giza. The Reïs Ahmed
went down to the river to give instructions to the dragoman for the dahabieh, and they set off in the motor-
caravans. Having crossed the Nile over the great Qasr al-
Nil bridge, they reached the road leading to the stupid
cones, from which forty centuries contemplate you.

"We'll arrive too soon," said the Reïs. "What do
you think about going upriver toward El Bahariya and
going through the sands to arrive at the Pyramids from
the west. That way, tomorrow morning, we'll see the sun
rise behind Cairo and the Sphinx. The view is worth the
trouble."

"Very well," Diana replied. "That way, we'll avoid
the Mena House and the Cook Agency."

Following the Reïs' directions, the Duchess, who
was at the wheel, steered the vehicle alongside the chain
of hills as far as Kerdasa, in the bed of a dried-up canal
half-filled with extremely fine sand, into which the
wheels sank to the thickness of the tires. Finally, the automobiles were able to emerge from that dust, and at ten
o'clock the moon rose, splendidly.

They were then in mid-desert; from the summit of
the hill-crest, the eyes embraced simultaneously, on the
left, the valley of the Nile and Cairo, whose minarets
sparkled in luminous lines on one side and dark ones on
the other. The Nile, still dark facing the city, was shining
to the north like a broad silver ribbon. The air was pure
and transparent; all the details of Masr El Kaïrah stood

out clearly, one after another, as the royal star climbed higher in the sky.

With gestures, Ahmed indicated the city's various monuments: "Slightly to the left, the Kam'a El Azhar, from which we've come; further away, on the horizon, those bright dots are the minarets of the tombs of the caliphs; further to the right, the citadel. Following the line of the ancient ramparts, there's the Darb El Sakiah, which leads to the El Meïdan souks. That square of sparkling minarets is the Kam'a ibu Touloun."

The spectacle was magical. The Oriental quarters, illuminated by the pale radiance, presented a sect straight out of the Thousand-and-One Nights. One expected to see an adorable peri gliding through the diamond-bright atmosphere, or a winged horse varying away the prince of dreams and the princess of poetry. All the details of Arab architecture, so various and so noble in its apparent disorder, appeared one after another, creating gradua-tions of hue ranging from the most delicate pink to the deepest violet. Toward the center, the verdure of the gar-den of the Ezbekieh and those of Kamil Pasha formed two patches of limpid emerald green, striped with black by the tall cypresses. The Nile, in all its splendor, was like an immense stream of mercury. Then the shadows shortened, as the rays fell more vertically.

"Turn around now," said Ahmed, "and look at the desert."

In that direction, a succession of gentle undulations becomes gradually more accentuated toward the south-west as the chain of the Libyan hills rose up. The aridity of the sand in the moonlight gives the impression of a snowy steppe, roseate white accentuated in places by a brutally violet amber. Close by, on the edge of the rocky chain, a brightly-illuminated cube projects the blue-tinted rays of its electricity far and wide. That is the Mena Hotel, and a procession of crawling ants is visible making its way toward that huge dice set on the sands. The air is so pure that burst of laughter and voices reach them.

The nasal sound of an accordion soon joins the voices.

Diana made an angry gesture. "More Cook tourists. Let's go!"

"They'll be here for a good three or four hours," said the Reïs. "What we ought to do is go toward Kerdasa and visit the pyramids of Abu Rawash, and come back to Giza via the desert. With your powerful autos, it's a small detour of no importance; we'll arrive at the pyramid of Cheops after these untimely folk have gone."

Diana surrendered the wheel to the chauffeur and got back into the vehicle. The excursion continued. "I've already see the pyramids of Giza," she said to the Reïs, "but not those of Abu Rawash. Are they interesting?"

"The largest one, in raw brick, which is imposing in its mass, has the rock itself for a nucleus. The nature of the materials and the calcareous sarcophagus seem to indicate an extreme antiquity. The other two pyramids, which are smaller, are unimpressive. Fortunately, that region doesn't have the celebrity of Giza, where we'd be harassed by the indigenes. Watch out for debris, driver— there are heaps of it everywhere."

The road was, indeed, becoming hazardous. The travelers got out of the vehicle, climbed a hill from which they would be able to see the grandiose monument, and examined the landscape.

Apart from the large pyramid, which loomed up enormously in the midst of a mass of rubble, there was complete desolation, like a dead world. The vague forms of walls, columns and porticos, all so worn and corroded, eaten away by the centuries, an architectural skeleton in the moonlight, chilled the heart.

"The Earth after the disappearance of humans," said Ormus.

A dog howled like a lunatic in the village; other dogs immediately replied.

"Go back," said the Duchess to the driver. "Wait with the autos. We're going to take a stroll through this nightmare."

"What!" said a hoarse but ironic voice, in bad English. "Carriages move without horses now? That oddity's all that was lacking!"

Everyone turned round. A phantom had just surged forth from an excavation, doubtless the familiar spirit of the dead world: an old man, almost naked, as bald as a kneecap, with a beard that would have made Moses or Michelangelo jealous, thin and bony limbs without the slightest appearance of flesh, and a skin shiny with dirt without any crust of dust.

They all considered the strange ascetic in bewilderment.

"Ha ha!" he sniggered. "Look at what civilization represents nowadays! What are you doing here? It's the domain of the dead—mine. Let the living stay away! Or, if they want a place, let them say so—there's no shortage of tombs in my domain."

"Who are you?" Adsum asked.

"Who am I? Less than nothing, but more than you. I'm human poverty. I've always existed, and I think I'm immortal."

"An Egyptian misanthrope!" said Diana. "That's not banal."

"You're mistaken, young woman. I'm no misanthrope. I love men, my brothers in stupidity, and women, my sisters in vice and turpitude—and the proof is that I haven't run away from you. Why should I avoid you, you who are bringing progress and liberty here—but perhaps not virtue and liberty? Ha ha! Liberty hamstrung by noble Albion! Virtue guided by a clergyman, with the Bible in one hand and a whip in the other."

"We're not English," said the Duchess. "We're American."

"Aha! The daughter of Noah who covers her father's nakedness."

"Punish this clown!" exclaimed the American woman.

"If that might amuse you. I have a hard skin, no longer having anything but skin. Have I come in search of you? You came to wake me up. I have a right and a duty to spit my scorn at you, males and females of a ridiculous and wicked world, a world in which people grow stupid in errors and lies. I've almost been human, but I've rejected that shame with horror. You ask who I am? I'm the scum, the mud, the pus of a rotten world! Hit me! Trample me underfoot. I'll infect you with my dirtiness, my ignominy, my virus. And now you know that such an abject being exists, go away! Get out! Let the dead rest in peace!"

He turned his back on them and went back into his hole.

The tourists, pensive and nonplussed, went back to their automobiles and took the road to Giza. They remained silent until the vehicles stopped in front of the pyramid of Cheops. The excursionists from the Mena Hotel had gone, and the Bedouins who, under the pretext of explaining the region of the tombs and acting as cicerones thereto, are as bothersome as mosquitoes, had gone back to their hovels, not expecting other visitors. The place was therefore free, and the visitors could dream in complete liberty.

The moon, now at the highest point of its course, illuminated the desert and the gigantic monuments as well as broad daylight, with the advantage that it was much cooler at this hour. Antal Fodor went to the vehicle to look for a scarf and wrapped the Duchess in it. A sepulchral silence reigned over the vast extent.

"Behold these proud sepulchers," said Ormus, "which have seen so many great events pass over thousands of years, and now have only the inexhaustible caravan for tourists for admirers."

"I anticipated another emotion," said Diana. "I expected to have the sensation of a recall of memory. For the second time, the Sphinx remains mute for me!"

"It's because your Double isn't here. The colossal tomb of Cheops was not visible for you, who resided in Thebes and only went out of it in order to be taken to the Valley of the Kings."

Diana, however, a trifle disillusioned, compared all that one imagines with the little that one encounters. Looking at the enchantment of Egypt at too close a range, that evening, she saw idols falling within her, breaking her dream, from which the obelisk had passed.

She thought, secretly, that love alone was a sovereign temple—which might crumble, but to be replaced, sooner or later, by another.

And the poor, melancholy Pharaoh's wife watched a shower of shooting stars in the African night, trying to catch sight of an invisible god winnowing those stars.

VII. A Little Life in Death

The Pharaoh's wife, with her horror of crowds and modernity, wanted to contemplate the pyramids and their forty centuries, and the desert, which had even more centuries, when there was no one else anyone around. Other women have different tastes, however, which do not incite them to flee their contemporaries.

At the same time as Diana, Adsum and Ormus, there was a joyful band of young Englishwomen in Cairo, with their boy-friends, all very young avid for pleasure, movement and gaiety. A sumptuous Hispano carried them along the white and duty road, silvered by the moonlight and the headlights, and they quickly found themselves in open country, where a few rare villas were asleep in the midst of centenarian gardens.

Already shining are the lights of the Mena, a palace constructed in the middle of the sands near the pyramids, which, realizing all the refinements of light and electricity, aliments a swimming-pool in its immense and marvelous garden, and lights it by means of artificial stars by night.

The brown vanished façade of the wooden hotel, in the Moorish style, is a genuine lacework, brightened at every window by little boxes of colorful geraniums. In front of the perron, bell-boys huddle, clad in broad bouffant trousers with red waistcoats embroidered with gold, a tarboosh or a turban coiffing their dark heads, hiding the unique tufts of hair remaining there, by means of which Mohammed pulls his faithful followers to him.

The joyous band gets out of the automobile. They go in search, in the vicinity of the Mena, of camels with purple and green saddles, camels that have necklaces of trinkets, and fetishes in quantity.

The large docile animals allow themselves to be mounted and led away by a bronzed guide, and the troupe sets off for the pyramids. They are visible, squat and mauve in the sapphire sky, gigantic, impressive in their grandeur and the majesty of straight and mysterious lines.

Ten minutes later, the bare-headed gallants and their female companions, with page-boy haircuts and short skirts, are able to contemplate the three colossal objects, constructed out of immense blocks of tone, at close range. By means of a few projections, the agile Bedouins, to whom a few piastres have been given, climb up to the summit; and people aggravated by travel literature yawn with admiration for the stone giants, a trifle stupid.

That evening, the moonlight inundated the desert as far as the eye can see. A warm breeze, perfumed by acacias, caressed the face. The tall silhouettes of the camels were outlined in darkness on the sand, the sky and the granite walls. A slender form, crouching in a corner, intrigued the genteel misses. It was a fortune-teller, and the merry group, in order to amuse themselves, interrogated her in turn.

Gravely, the young sorceress traced fantastic signs in the dust of the sand and the moon, in order to unveil the future, with her fingers of bronze with silver rigs. Then, delectable with local color, she developed her predictions, with English words picked up here and there, to the great joy of all that youth intoxicated by all kinds of hope and the heady scent of the flowers in the gardens of the Mena—which, beneath the twinkling of innumerable stars, sent forth their seductive magic.

Then all the adolescents go back to the Mena. In the background, in the vast palm-plantation, nimble American women are trotting on horseback, accompanied by their current boy-friends, and in the swimming-pool, other young women are bathing. Their slender bodies, clad in short pink swimming costumes that strip them bare in the bewitching shadows—without any blonde or brunette secret animality—are reminiscent of naiads or fairies. Their harmonious gestures, under the moon on that beautiful night, have something eternal about them.

Are they the returned shades of the marvelous princesses of an Egypt of long ago? No, just pretty girls frolicking under the gaze of the same nocturnal divinity—and beside those princesses in flower, the pyramids are stupid.

VIII. The Smile of the Sphinx

While chatting, the Duchess and her companions had gone around the great pyramid of Cheops, and before them stood the enigmatic and colossal Sphinx.

"Master," Ormus asked Adsum, "have you nothing particular to tell us about the Pharaoh Khufu, the fourth-dynasty king of Egypt who had the largest of the pyramids built?"

"No, in that epoch I was not in Egypt—but I can tell you about the Sphinx, for I assisted in its construction."

There as a pause. Ormus and Ahmed were already sitting on the sand. Pharaoh's wife perched like a goat on a block of stone, and Adsum, still standing up, began.

"I was then a servant in the temple of Horus, one of the Father's names. As you can see, through the ages, I find myself again what I was thousands of years ago: a worshiper of the Sun.

"When, exiled by the defeat of his kingdom of Arafista, the great Mehnes[20] penetrated into Egypt and stopped on the banks of the Nile, this region was only inhabited by a few African tribes who had come down from the high plateaux, and populations originating, like

---

[20] This name, more commonly rendered Menes, was attributed to the founder of the first dynasty by the Egyptian historian Manetho; it was, however, Herodotus who named the hypothetical first pharaoh as the founder of Memphis. The rest of the story is improvised, although Menes was credited with a son named Athothis, whose name in vaguely echoed in Adsum's story.

him, from India. The only weapons those tribes had were slings and clubs. Mehnes, although defeated, was at the head of an army of twenty thousand men, with weapons of iron and bronze, knowing the use of the bow and the lance. He defeated the resistant tribes easily, submitted them to slavery, and founded the first Egyptian city; Mehnes-Phi.

"The son of a civilization that was already old, Mehnes soon understood that he had arrived in a land with a great future. The Nile, although it was far, in that epoch, from being what it is today, carried masses of humus extracted from the high plateaux of Central Africa. He created an autocratic absolute monarchy, and, in order to achieve that result, declared himself the son of the Sun. He built a great temple to his Father, and instituted a clergy, appointed by him, which he initially recruited from among his military leaders. The high priest, Osthi-Amon, a man avid for honors and wealth, myself, Amaheh, and three other Levites, formed the whole of the clergy.

"Osthi-Amon immediately seized the immense authority that he was able to acquire over an ignorant and superstitious people, all the more easily because Mehnes thought of nothing but increasing the size of his empire and submitting the surrounding ribs to its yoke. Leaving the internal government to Osthi-Amon, who had his full confidence, he extended his conquests, in one direction beyond the Nile—which then had only a fifth of its present width, while the sea bathed the foothills of the Libyan and Arabian mountains. It was, therefore, toward the south, most of all, that the monarch extended his domination. Building cities and instituting governments. The interbreeding of Hindu and African races formed a new race, which, after two thousand years, acquired a definitive type.

"Between conquests, Mehnes returned triumphantly to Mehnes-Phi. That name was the badge of its founder, and meant "city of Menes." Every time, the clergy, which, under the impulsion of its leader, had increased prodigiously in size—without causing Mehnes any anxiety—exalted the glory and the so-called divinity of the Master. That adroit means, pushing the Pharaoh's pride to the point of dementia, permitted the high priest to increase his fortune and his power.

"It was then that, in order to flatter the Pharaoh's vanity, Osthi-Amon suggested to him that he leave an imperishable monument to is glory: to sculpt outside the city, on the first buttresses of the mountain, an enormous rock overlooking the sea. Mehnes accepted his divinity. The Nile forced the river-dwellers to rest for three months, permitting the employment of the entire population, during that lapse of time, to undertake gigantic labors. The surrounding mountains furnished inexhaustible quarries of granite and limestone. A few temples and the Royal Palace were sketches out in the capital, and under the direction of the great sculptor Am-Ahoury, the monument to Mehnes was carved.

"In that epoch, the sea came all the way to the foot of the Libyan mountains, and Memphis—to use its present name—was a seaport; not a very deep port, in truth, but sufficient for the flat-bottomed boats then in use, and of which the dahabieh of today is merely a enlarged and improved replica.

"For eleven years, the stone-carvers worked on the statue of the man-god; for eleven years, more than ten thousand men toiled over that formidable, truly splendid task, but the stone block was not yet tall enough to crown the head of the colossus with the royal and divine emblems—which is to say, with a sort of tiara forming a solar disk coupled with lotus flowers and the double serpent. That part of the monument was carved separately, and in order to put it in place, an inclined plane was established, rising all the way to the summit of the statue's head.

"The work had reached that point when, one evening, Osthi-Amon, whose secretary and friend I was, summoned me to him. Then he made me party to a grandiose project intended to free the church of Horus from all authority and give him supremacy over the Pharaoh. This is what it involved.

"Mehnes had five wives. His favorite was the daughter of an Arab chief, conquer by force. Her name was Mekri; she was very beautiful, but stupid and exceedingly superstitious. The high priest had obtained an absolute empire over her, and it was on that domination that he had established his plan. Mekri had given her husband two sons and a daughter; the older son, Atahot, was only seven years old. In case of the Pharaoh's death, therefore, Mekri was assured a long guardianship, and, in consequence, a regency of which Osthi-Amon would be the absolute master

"This was the high priest's thinking: the Pharaoh's boundless vanity made him believe in his own divine essence, not only in spirit but in body. Osthi-Amon created, in his own interest, the hypothesis of the Double, with the indefinite conservation of the envelope in which the spirit could persist until the day of its absorption into the ancestral divinity: Horus, the Sun.

"For that imperishable sheath, that Double, an indestructible habitation was required in which the defunct individual was placed in an upright position, surrounded by everything that he needed to await the great deliverance. A Pharaoh, however, merited something better. Within the very head of the statue, therefore, a funerary chamber had been hollowed out, which a gigantic miter would cover and seal hermetically.

"The statue and the mortuary chamber were complete. The head-dress, an immense block of granite twenty cubits high, enormously heavy, had been carved in place on rollers and a inclined plane. The genius of Am-Ahoury had established the ensemble so well that a few blows of a sledgehammer would suffice, on the day of the Pharaoh's burial, to expel the wedges retaining the miter, in order that it would slide and fit into the notch designed to receive it.

"A few days later, Mehnes was to make a triumphal entry into Memphis. The inauguration of the statue, cleared of the scaffolding and a part of the inclined plane, was included in the program of celebrations. 'This is what your role will be,' the high priest said to me. 'Pay close attention, and don't omit a single detail.'

"Minutely, he explained his plan, which was admirably conceived, but had one basic flaw. Osthi-Amon believed himself to be the absolute master of the Pharaoh's wife; he was only half-right, for I had been her lover for three years, and she only seemed to be devoted to the high priest in order to elevate me.

"The great day arrived. A veil had been extended before the statue in such a fashion as to mask it on the side of the city. At sunrise, all the trumpets sounded; the zithers and drums made a solemn noise, while the Pharaoh, the prestigious Mehnes, on a magnificent chariot, surrounded by a multitude of chiefs and warriors, advanced. When he was close, the veil fell, and the Sphinx appeared to the eyes of the monarch and his court.

"How beautiful it was, that monster twenty-eight meters high, with its impassive and sublime mask of the omnipotent autocrat, more divine than human, in that monstrous animal form. And I, who was due to play a terrible role that day, felt a glacial chill run through me at the sight of it; for me most of all, that mask, as impassive as Destiny, had an expression of formidable irony. However, the entire clergy, after a genuflection before the living, eternal god, was to file before the Pharaoh, dazzled by his own grandeur.

"The sculptor-architect advanced toward the Pharaoh, prostrated himself, and said: 'O Son of the Sun, your portrait is greater than you in its dimensions, but smaller than you beside your glory!'

"The high priest had approached the Pharaoh and spoken to him in a low voice. Mehnes nodded his approval; then Osthi-Amon raised the artist to his feet and embraced him. 'Am-Ahoury,' he said, 'you are henceforth the foremost in Memphis, and you will have lodgings and a table in the temple of the gods that you have so marvelously reproduced. Look, Am-Ahoury, look closely at your masterpiece, for you will never see it again!'

"In response to a signal, the temple guards took possession of the artist, seated him in a chariot, and bore him away in triumph. The architect never saw his work again; his eyes were closed forever in order that, being blind, he could never make another similar masterpiece. Thus, heaped with gratitude and honors, Am-Ahoury ended his days deprived of light in the temple of the Sun!

"Now, the high priest and the Pharaoh mounted the framework in order to visit the funerary chamber, while I and two of the most vigorous of the temple guards surrounded the granite miter. Mehnes and Osthi-Amon descended into the chamber.

"Then, in response to a signal, before the high priest had emerged, as we had agreed, leaving the Omnipotent to meditate briefly on his eternal Double, my co-conspirators withdrew the masses of iron and simultaneously removed the wedges retaining the enormous stone miter. It shook, slid with a thunderous noise, and sealed the Pharaoh's tomb. Then, with great cries of triumph, I proclaimed the glory of Mehnes and the high-priest Osthi-Amon, who had entered voluntarily into celestial apotheosis together, into immortality.

"The Pharaoh and the high priest having been swallowed up in the bosom of Horus, within sight of all the people, by virtue of their own final order, power came into the hands of the regent—and, in consequence, into mine, thanks to the subjugated mind of Queen Mekri.

"We married Athotis to his sister as soon as he was twelve years old, and I took care to stupefy him by means of anticipated enjoyments. I was, therefore, the true master of Egypt.

"The centuries have passed over the ironic monster; the miter has crumbled away, strewing its debris around the statue. The desert wind has carried away the ashes of the Pharaoh and his high priest. Only the granite sphinx remains.

"Its human face speaks of intelligence, its breasts of love, its claws of combat; its wings are faith, the dream and the hope of human flight into the heavens; its bovine flanks counsel labor down here.[21] But you now know why that animal god, nibbled by the Sun and the wind,

---

[21] This description does not match the great sphinx of Giza, but includes features typical of Greek sphinxes.

has always had its enigmatic smile. It has devoured the man who was perhaps the greatest of the Pharaohs. Does it hope to survive humankind on the dead globe, alone?"

IX. Symptoms of Saturation

From Laouat El Aryan onwards, the ultimate buttresses of the Libyan mountain chain come to melt into
the sands, and the banks of the Nile are already encased.
There is a cultivable strip between the Nile and the
mountain.

The travelers paused in Saqqara, wanting to explore
on foot the enormous quantity of pyramids and mastabas
garnishing that region, entirely populated by the dead.
The pyramids, of several of which only the location can
be perceived, number eighteen. Only one is veritably
interesting—the most ancient and best-conserved. It is
the so-called step-pyramid, the tomb of King Djoser of
the third dynasty. As for the mastabas, they are innumerable.

Although pyramids were consecrated to kings and
Pharaohs—which is to say, emperors—mastabas were
the sepulchers of aristocrats or important functionaries.
Steles relate their names and ranks, giving information
about the civic life of the times, and completing the mu-
ral inscriptions of temples and royal tombs.

But what is a mastaba?

A mastaba has strong analogies with the little chapels of modern Christian churches. It consisted of a vestibule giving access to a chapel where the stele was
placed, and on the walls, the most important events of
the life of the deceased individual were recorded in
paintings. Externally, the mastaba had the appearance of
a sharply-inclined pyramid truncated four or five meters
from its base; the terrace surmounting it was tiled on the
sides inclined toward the north, east or south, but never

to the west. The door-frame and granite portico were sometimes ornamented by pillars supporting an entablature on which "the sign of the tomb" was engraved. In the center of the terrace was a shaft, its depth depending on the location—for it needed to attain a depth within the rock of twenty or thirty meters. There, a sloping vestibule contained the sarcophagus, which, by that means, was placed beneath the chapel. The whole was cleverly hidden, in order to escape tomb-robbers.

A pathway through these tombs and pyramids formed a veritable labyrinth.

"People in Europe seem to be astonished by this strange religion, which made Egyptian life into a constant preoccupation with death," said Antal Fodor. "It was justified by belief in the Double, which forced the living to take care of an envelope that they had to recover intact for a further incarnation. We moderns, who do not have the same belief, nevertheless employ similar practices, limited solely by fortune. Does one not see, in the cemeteries of Europe or America, poor people surrounding with pious care the earth that covers their dead? Centuries have passed, but something of their beliefs still remains."

"Certainly," Adsum replied, "and I find therein a vague memory of preceding incarnations. Do we not see, in our day, trees, rocks and springs edified under the labels of saints or madonnas? The ignorant soul evolves, is renewed, but maintains the same errors and the same superstitions."

"Let's go," said Diana. "These necropolises, which are the great attraction of pilgrimages, weigh upon me like a leaden mantle. Let's allow our spirits to relax. For my part, I feel the need to see a little greenery, and I'd like an excursion to the great oasis or Lake Birket-el-

Keroun. Since the episode of the Sphinx I find all these monuments repulsive. It seems to me that these masses of granite conceal a multitude of crimes."

"Even if they don't all hide political crimes," said Adsum, "their construction nevertheless cost the lives of thousands of people."

"How?" asked Diana.

"The great projects were carried out during the flooding of the Nile, imposed on the inhabitants in the form of forced labor. The laborers were fed, but not paid—the construction workers, that is; the quarrymen and miners were recruited by civil and military condemnations. All punishment consisted of years in the galleys, as oarsmen, or in the quarries. When a Pharaoh had need of strong arms, severity was increased and the slightest misdemeanor led to forced labor. They were all treated very harshly, poorly-nourished—and as the work of laying foundations in the mud led to fevers and epidemics, I can certify that every temple, or even the erection of an obelisk, cost the lives of thousands of men. The pyramid of Cheops, which put millions of arms to work for ten years, caused so much depopulation that a famine decimated the third that remained."

"Then let's go, quickly!" said Diana. "I'm positively in haste to get far away from all these tombs. How far is it to the Lake of Horns?"

"About forty kilometers—two or three hours' travel through the desert. We can have lunch on one of the islands."

X. Arab Hospitality

The excursion to the Lake of Horns—the popular name of Birket-el-Keroun—was not without incident. Scarcely had the travelers covered a few kilometers than the kamsin rose, not as a tempest but sufficiently to hinder the progress of the automobiles and force them to stop. In spite of the hermetic closure of the hoods, further protected by damp cloths, the sand penetrated nevertheless and choked the engines.

It was the same inside the vehicles, and Diana interrogated the Father anxiously.

"There's no absolute peril," Adsum replied. "It's only a sandstorm, frequent in the region. In a couple of hours, at the most, we can proceed with a careful cleaning of the machines, and set off again thereafter. In the meantime, let's wrap up our faces as best we can, and summon up all our philosophy."

Indeed, after an hour, the wind dropped. When Diana's vehicle had been cleaned, she got into it with the two mages, and the servants stayed behind to restore the other two vehicles to working order.

After a fairly long journey, they arrived at Taniyeh, the nearest village—not very large, but in sufficient communication with Europeans for the travelers to find what they needed there. The Sheikh, Able El Massaoud, had one of the principal fishing concessions with regard to the lake. Very rich and well-educated, he hastened to make the three travelers welcome, especially once he discovered, from the Reïs, the status of the American woman. He offered them the honors of his house and introduced them to his harem.

170

While the Duchess was entertained by the Sheikh's wife, the great Arab lord and the two mages installed themselves in what Able El Massaoud called "the drawing room" and ate a few local foodstuffs, which were exquisite, not without first having done honor to the "mézé."

Mézé consists of a quantity of small *hors-d'oeuvre*: stuffed vine-leaves; lamb sausages scented with herbs, grilled and crushed into little balls; and aubergine salad, strongly spiced. The whole is served on a large tray shaped like a flower or featuring some design. The tray constitutes a kind of puzzle that can be separated into a host of small plates of various forms, from which everyone can take the preferred foodstuff according to his taste.

The beverage accompanying the mézé is strongly alcoholic, with a taste of aniseed, known as raki. It is consumed in silence, almost religiously, in delicate little glasses, elegant in form. After the mézé comes an enormous fish served whole, about two meters long. The indigenes call it *fa'ach*, and the sheikh's guests appreciated it greatly. It was presented on a long wooden latter, cooked on the grill, seasoned with a very pungent sauce and sprinkled with lemon juice.

Diana ate in the harem. It consisted of only one wife, a very pretty Armenian, whom the Sheikh had saved during one of the massacres frequent between Turks and Armenians. He had snatches her from a burning house where she was lying unconscious among her dead relatives. She was then thirteen years of age. Her savior had married her, and she was happy with him, even though he was twenty years older than her.

"There's to be a big fishing-trip the day after tomorrow," she told Diana. "If you want to see it, I'll ask my husband to bring it forward a day. It's very curious."

"Gladly—we're in no hurry. We're in Egypt to study that which, in the lives of the people, survives over time through political changes."

"In that case, I can assure you that our method of fishing has scarcely changed since the remotest times."

XI. An Egyptian Spiritualist

While the two new friends exchanged confidences, Able El Messaoud had, once the meal as over, taken the two mages into what he called, in the European manner, his "studio." Not without astonishment, the mages found a library principally composed of books on occultism and philosophy. The Sheikh—who, like all bibliophiles, seemed proud of his books—drew their attention to a collection of periodicals and pamphlets relating to magnetism and spiritualism.

"This proves that I'm a true Oriental," he said. "Although I'm cheerful by nature, the great mystery of life and death has always fascinated me, and I take a great interest in studies intended to prove the immortality of the spirit and its manifestations beyond the grave. Perhaps you're indifferent to that, though."

"Entirely to the contrary," replied Antal Fodor, enthusiastically, "since the objective of our voyage to Egypt is research of a psychic order. We are not laymen, and might be able to help you."

"God! From all this mess of papers I can only extract hypothesis, not certainties. I've studied all these occult authors, French and otherwise, with all the more determination because I'm searching for conviction. There's no doubt that a fluidic force exists, emanating from ourselves, and a fluidic force emanating from the unknown—but where does the latter come from? That's the question that no one, thus far, has been able to resolve."

"We'll offer you a hypothesis," Adsum said, "that has the advantage over the others of a greater probability. Present-day spiritualism rests on two recognized and proven facts: the levitation of tables and various other objects, and the existence of mediums. The first of those causes is in contradiction to the law of gravity, and in order to explain it, it's necessary to contravene that law—which seems, however, to rule the worlds.

"That force of levitation, escaping a law that we're accustomed to recognize, has to be explained as an action of the fluidic force emanating from ourselves. It is concentrated in a will-power that dominates matter and its laws. We have a false idea of matter in considering it as inert mass; matter is alive. The pebbles on the road and the sand of the desert are alive, since they are transformed; they have been part of an organic body, and they will be again.

"In nature, time does not exist. Humans imagine that they are creating immortality, by building pyramids and carving a granite Sphinx in the rock: a question of time; although it might taken then thousand years, a day will come when the sphinx and the pyramids will disappear under the action of the ages and those mountains of stone will become once again what they were before: sand. And that sand will return to the oceans in order to agglomerate again, to become animal or mineral, whatever; but inactive mater does not exist.

"As for fluidic forces, they are innumerable; every body emits waves, and suggestion proves that a human being, the greatest psychic concentralizer, is, in consequence, the most powerful emitter of these psychic fluids. What are called mediums are humans who, by means of a natural gift and by severe study of the concentration of thought, are able to impose their will on other people by means of mental suggestion. They can also concentrate the fluidic forces of others, and create in that fashion a force that is manifest externally: the displacement of objects, apports, collective illusions. Is there, in all that, a connection to the beyond? No, for it would be ridiculous for a spirit of the astral purity to lend itself to such puerile manifestations.

"However, a few facts seem to prove the contrary, and it would be absurd to reject them without scientific investigation, when they can be explained by one simple fact: at the moment of death, the spirit—which is to say, the psychic 'self,' the thinking self, leaves the body that it has borrowed during an existence, and which will return to the universal for further transformation. The fluid spirit, dispossessed of its senses—which are for the living nothing but means of manifestation for the brain, the motor of sensation—still exists. It remains in the universe at the exact location from which it emerged from its terrestrial envelope, for the Earth, in its dual movement of axial and orbital rotation had left it behind.

"Spirits that have not evolved in the course of their terrestrial passage—and for how many is that the case?—no longer know where they are, or what they are. Wandering, lost in the astral immensity, an indescribable terror brings them back to the Earth where they lived, where they will live again in order to reach the degree of evolution that it is necessary for them to acquire. Most of the time—not to say always—it is those spirits that manifest themselves through the intermediary of mediums, and their manifestations of ignorance can only be uninteresting or stupid.

"In addition to these inferior spirits there are others: pure ones, having rejected the material envelope forever, who live the fluidic life of angels—not those represented to us by religious paintings, but immaterial, invisible beings, perhaps nourishing themselves on light.

"How far does the strangeness of conceptions in the creations of the terrestrial soul extend? Think about the multiplicity of forms, of modes of existence, of reproduction. All that the fantasy of a pen can imagine will find its counterpart in the scale of beings; everything is kneaded from the same clay, everything nourishes itself on the same matter, and yet, everything differs in its aspect and character.

"Since there are fluidic forces on Earth, then, why should there not be entirely fluid beings? Magnetism, electricity, light and sound all propagate by means of waves. And what is a wave? An unconscious are active force? To act is to be, to have a will. So?"

"So, humans seek..."

"Around us, within us, millions of beings that we cannot see, but which exist, are acting, living, dying. There are colors that our eyes do not see; and rays, invisible to us, that have an influence upon us. The entire universe is nothing but a formidable vibration, in which the enormous in juxtaposed with the infinitesimal, which it needs in order to be. Can we deny the marvelous and the supernatural, since the marvelous surrounds us and the supernatural of today might be the natural of tomorrow?"

"What do you conclude?" asked the Sheikh. Is spiritualism—by which I mean the communication of the living with the dead—possible?"

"Possible, but, as I've told you, uninteresting, since the dead are as ignorant as you, and must instruct themselves on the astral plane, or undergo numerous reincarnations on Earth."

"But can a superior intelligence not communicate with the living?"

"It is a very considerable suffering for it. Moreover, it is necessary for it to make use of the intermediary of a medium, who is almost always insincere, even unknowingly—hence, uncertainty as to the truth for the interrogator. Everything about this matter is complex.

"Is not the human spirit inherently complicated? Is it not completely different during sleep, when one can accomplish actions that one could not think of doing in a waking state? When I recall my memories of youth, I remember a dream that pursued me obstinately: I was walking perpendicularly, and it only required a slight pressure of the foot or he hand to make me progress. Was that a reminiscence of another world?

"In any case, our diurnal spirit is often subject to a duplication; when you are reading, while your mind consciously scans the lines, your mind is thinking about something else. Are there no examples of thoughts doubling themselves under the influence of certain urgencies? Bonaparte dictated several letters simultaneously; a chess player can play several games at the same time. The mystery that reigns over all nature reigns within ourselves.

"To return to our subject, I believe in the possibility of fluidic beings on our globe, created by the Earth, like the rest of terrestrial humankinds."

"What do you think about metempsychosis?"

"It seems to indicate an animal progression. Progression, says the moral mentality, if there is reward, regression if there is punishment. But who is the judge? Let us admit that I have been an animal; what noble action has that animal been able to accomplish in order to become a man?

"The mentality of beasts is imagined to be inferior. That is false, since the animal makes provision for its shelter, its nourishment and its reproduction; it performs the same duties as a human, with a few additional qualities. Humans, endowed with intelligence, generally do things that can harm them; animals do not. Humans kill for pleasure; animals kill in order to live or defend themselves. Humans have invented laws to shackle their liberty; animals life freely, and if they submit to humans it is often by necessity, and their masters are then obliged to lodge and nourish them.

"Why refuse animal, or plants, a psychology, and even a language? Humans have judged it simpler to appropriate a fluidic part, the spirit.

"In sum, let us never say, in an affirmative manner, 'I believe.' Let us say simply, 'I suppose.'"

The Sheikh listened respectfully to the old man, his guest.

XII. Lake Birket-El-Keroun

It was on the Birket-El-Keroun, or Lake of Horns, fifty kilometers long by ten wide, between four and five meters deep, alimented by a few small streams descending from the Gabel Gadala, whose name is derived from its shape, that the fishing expedition mentioned by Madame Messaoud was to take place. The Sheikh had given orders for the preparations to be advanced by a day, in order that his guests could take part in it.

The flat-bottomed boats that served for fishing, being the only ones capable of navigating over the depths covered in reeds and papyrus, were widely scattered; all night long the Arabs had labored to gather them together and clear a path through the aquatic plants in order to allow them to reach the middle of the lake, where the fishing would be done.

One of the vessels had been fitted out with a carpet and cushions; Diana, Adsum, Ormus and the Sheikh took their places in it, and they all set out. In the prow of the boat a large stove had been lit, on which odorant herbs were burning, in order to drive away the mosquitoes and combat the un-balsamic scent of the mud and rotting vegetation that circled the edges. In the middle of the lake the atmosphere was purer, for the desert commenced on the far side.

When the sun emerged above the mountains, the boats were immediately immobilized, and a clear voice rose up, intoning the morning prayer: "*La ilaha ill'Allah, oua Mohammed resul Allah!*" All the sailors, standing up with their heads bowed, murmured the prayer.

The homage rendered by those primitive men to the god who is god, the one who has no image, who has no name but is the Father of all—and, doubtless, to his representative, the Sun, fecundator of the globe—beneath the vast sky, profoundly blue, in the middle of that expanse of water, was simple but imposing.

Adsum and Antal Fodor exchanged glances, which meant: "Of all religions, this is the one that will be most easily assimilated to ours."

The boatmen had picked up their short oars with broad blades. Seated in the oriental fashion in the bow of the command-boat, the Sheikh gave orders. Each vessel carried six men, four oarsmen and two fishermen, the first armed with a long trident, the second with a dagger held in a bracelet attached to the left wrist. The man with the dagger was naked save for a loincloth.

The captain steered to windward, in order that the smoke would be driven back over the boat; the mosquitoes, which were flying around the boats in millions, drew away slightly. The Arabs did not appear to be inconvenienced by that invasion, but everyone in the command-boat was tightly wrapped in muslin.

On the Sheikh's order the boats drew apart, tracing a semicircle, and at a prearranged signal, al the rowers began to beat the water with their oars, uttering shrill and prolonged cries.

Suddenly, a long white furrow appeared in the surface, and then many others. The cries increased, and the fish, disturbed and bewildered, raced back and forth in all directions, colliding with one another. There was a flash and then an impact; the trident-bearer had hurled his weapon violently, like a javelin.

Leaning over the edge, the man with the dagger followed the wounded fish with his eyes; the shallow depth of the lake did not permit the victim to hide. The long shaft of the trident agitated the surface, indicting the spot where the animal was struggling.

The propitious moment having arrived, the diver leapt into the water and swam toward the wounded fish, turning it skillfully, seized the shaft of the trident with one hand, and sliced the belly of the fish from end to end with the other. It was an enormous "hout," almost two meters in length.

The dry clicking of tridents, launched with force, was audible on all sides, and such was the fishermen's skill that they rarely missed. When that did happen, by virtue of bad luck, laughter and mocking gibes rained down on the unfortunate who then had to dive in to recover his weapon. That was not without danger for him, because a thrash of the tail of one of the enormous fish could stun a fisherman, and sometimes drown him.

They continued for an hour, and then the Sheikh gave the signal to return. They brought back at least three thousand kilos of fish, which would be distributed equitable to the crowd.

"Aren't you curious to see the ruins of ancient Diong-Sies?" asked Madame Messaoud. "It's a two-hour journey in the automobile, and we'd be back in time for lunch."

The Duchess understood that the amiable woman was trying to remain in her company for as long as possible, and would, moreover, be delighted to make an excursion by auto, which she had not yet had an opportunity to do. She gave instructions to Henri, her French cook, who was to assist the Sheikh's people, and then they all set off for Case-Aeroum, which is the Egyptian name of the ancient Greek colony.

All that remains of the ancient city of Dionysius are a few formless masses of debris and the ruins of two temples, whose outline can still be made out. In an hour, they had seen it all; in spite of the reminder of her anterior life and the melancholy that emanates from the debris of the past that looms up at every step on Egyptian soil, the Duchess, accustomed to the "businesslike" tempo of the states of the Union, could not assimilate herself to that life, which had so little affinity with her own.

Antal Fodor felt similar impressions himself. Only Adsum did not miss a single detail. He was joyful in sniffing out and rediscovering the trail of ancient life.

They made the return journey and, as the Sheikh's wife had anticipated, arrived in time to sit down at table—and the meal was exceedingly cheerful. In the depths of their hearts, however, was a hidden regret, for they all sensed the approach of the moment of separation: of those little deaths of which life is composed.

XIII. Intellectual Domination

From Tanisch to Tersch and from Tersch to Medinet-El-Fayoum one encounters the same sequence of little villages buried like nests in the exuberant verdure of gardens and fields that promise a fine harvest. At Tersch they had crossed the railway line leading to Ebchoual, a modern anachronism in that region of the old world.

From Medinet, they set a course for Harouarah; there was a pyramid there that it was necessary to see, for it is one of the most interesting, from the viewpoint of its mode of construction. It was built with enormous unfired bricks disposed around a nucleus of natural rock twelve meters high. It is the tomb of Amenemhat II; the Pharaoh reposes there is a great sandstone sarcophagus, with the body of his wife, Neferouptah, beside him in a tiny coffin. The funerary chapel, with its annexes, comprises such a mass of constructions that one arrives there through a veritable maze-perhaps the famous labyrinth cited by Herodotus and Strabo.

For several kilometers, more tombs. Some distance from Harouarah, the pyramids of Illahoum and Ousirteren. Until then they had been traveling through Fayoum, the best-irrigated and most fertile region in the Nile valley, the most marvelous land in the world. The roads were bordered by clumps of acacias and black poplars, and, tall, rigid and bushy cypresses loomed up like obelisks of verdure. In the villages there as a veritable orgy of colors, so abundant were flowers: roses, jasmines, myrtles and arbutus mingled there like a veritable perfumed brushwood. Then there were plantations of bananas, almonds, oranges, figs, date-palms, lemons and pomegranates, not to mention indigenous fruits. It is always necessary to remember the nahea, whose little fruits taste like apples, and the gechtah with the thick cream.

Egypt! A land blessed by the gods; a veritable paradise on earth. The indigenes, finding life easy, allow themselves to live without cares, indifferent to the idea of fatherland, and long accustomed, moreover, to live under supervision, with the support of an age-old philosophy that submits to effects without debating their causes. Even the passage of the sumptuous automobiles did not excite either the curiosity or the envy of people indifferent to progress, who had remained the same for ten thousand years. Can they be shaken out of that indifference? Will one then see those children of old Egypt, who already pile into cinemas, wearing shoes on sidewalks, with felt hats or bowlers? Who can tell? Albion is a salesman!

Now, the three vehicles were parked side by side, and the servants were buy with the cooking and housekeeping, while Diana and the three men were chatting.

"Another two days," Adsum said, "and we'll be entering the Valley of the Kings."

"And you'll find 'our' tombs there?"

"Yes, my Daughter. Fortunately, they have not yet been discovered. Lord Carnarvon was mistaken, for he mistook the false one for the true."

"These Pharaohs are astonishing; their greatest concern during their lives was to think about the conservation of their Double, their endurance."

"The consequence of an incommensurable vanity!"

"And that will always be the case: all is vanity. As the Latin saying has it, *Vanitas vanitatum, omnia vanitas.*[22] The people of today are the same as those of yesterday, and it is this cult of the Double that has created the mania for the imperishable. Do you recall the mask of Amenothis IV, of which one sees reproductions everywhere? It's the face of a degenerate, for these Pharaohs can never have ruled effectively. They were playthings in the hands of priests or clever ministers."

"There is only one kind of domination," said Adsum, "the only one that can subsist throughout the centuries: intellectual domination—and that's why religions are so powerful. Humankind does not know how to march without a guide."

"And we are bringing it a new religion," Diana added, "in a spirit of progress: the Flower of Truth."

"Thanks to obligatory elementary education," Ormus said, "children could, if well-directed, prepare a luminous future for us. But they have lost faith, dispute dogmas, and do not answer to anyone except those who flatter their interest. An evil wind is blowing over the world; egotism is individual instead of being collective; no one thinks about anyone but himself!"

"So it is our duty," said Adsum, severely, "to put our apostolic devotion at the service of humankind, to fight narrow egotism to the death, for a start. Today, thanks to you, my Daughter, we have an ally of the greatest strength: money. I sometimes hear you pronounce infamous words, Ormus; you too have been infected by the spirit of the twentieth century. You want what people have always wanted: enjoyment. Enjoyment! What folly—what material satisfaction can match

---

[22] "Vanity of vanities, all is vanity"—the first words of the Old Testament book of *Ecclesiastes*, often quote in Latin by virtue of their use by the Roman Church.

spiritual satisfaction? What flash of gourmand or sensual pleasure can match the hours of the joy of thought? Age, you think, my children, imposes that wisdom upon me. Perhaps—but I sense within me a psychic plenitude previously unexperienced. That effect, you will feel too, and like me, you will regret the time wasted in base satisfactions. All in all, it doesn't matter. So long as I am with you, Ormus, I shall think and act for you."

"We're like the Christians' holy trinity," said the Duchess, laughing, "and you are the Father."

"Great faith moves toward women, and the spirit takes last place. The religion of the Madonna has replaced the antique Venus."

Ormus added: "But it's still the same idolatry, and lust hides modestly beneath the mystic veils. I prefer the antique lust of the ancients, which was simultaneously art and beauty."

On that conclusion, everyone retired to the automobiles. In the billionairess's motor-caravan, however, Diana repeated the young Mage's final words—and dreamed.

XIV. A Billionairess Afflicted by Ennui

At sunrise, after breakfast, they got under way again, leaving Abukir and its isolated mountain of Gabel-Gadala—which forms a natural pyramid between the Nile and the gorge of Mahouan—behind to the left. Avoiding all the small localities scattered along the great river, they went along the base of the Gabel, between the mount and the Bahr—i.e., river—Yousouf. They crossed over it in order to have lunch in Fechn.

Fechn, which now has a railways station, was once on the bank of the Nile, as evidenced by the remains of a dock, called Hippone, and its rather considerable ruins, extending to the modern town. Their ensemble can be seen from the terrace of the Hipponia House.

A Thomas Cook tour-party was swarming in front of the temple of Sekhmet. In the pure air, deflected by the screen of the mountain, the explanations of the cicerone could be heard, but not understood.

"They'll be there for two hours," said the Reïs. "We can eat tranquilly."

"Listen," said Diana. "I want to play a trick on these importunate tourists. Go with Henri to the kitchens of the Hipponia and stock up on provisions, taking everything, so that there'll be nothing left to eat when they get here."

The hotelier protested, not wanting to leave his stores empty, but Diana possessed the golden key that open all doors, and the little caravan, in spite of the indigestion of bankrupt stones, set out again for Abydos. Diana, distracted by an intimate preoccupation, smiled, and said things that were slightly foolish, momentarily amused by the joke she had played on the flock of tourists.

Old Egypt is a grandiose, monotonous cemetery. Diana was beginning to get seriously weary of debris, pyramids, necropolises, hieroglyphs and venerable heaps of rubble, almost all identical. The Reïs proposed a halt at the ruins of Till-El-Amarna, but the Pharaoh's wife decided to cross the Nile and to go upriver as far as the road to the great oasis. Why not admit that she was tired? She wanted a little solitude *à deux*. Adsum reminded her of St. John Chrysostom, the critic of dancing and free love when she was the Empress Eudoxia. This overlong excursion in the company of a man she desired, whom the continuous close proximity of Adsum and Ahmed prevented her from drawing to the subtle moment that her heart secretly desired, seemed tedious to her.

Used to seeing everyone yield to her caprice, she was astonished that the Mage was showing so little urgency to force her surrender. Her anterior lives had awoken within her the voluptuous mentality of Cleopatra and Eudoxia, exciting her imagination and her senses. She was in a hurry to reach the Valley of the Kings. She anticipated that when she and Ormus rediscovered their Doubles, that encounter would lead to a less platonic union. Since the impetuous kiss on Long Island, Diana had never been able to be alone with Ormus, who seemed to be avoiding a tête-à-tête on Adsum's orders.

They crossed over the Nile again, therefore, and abandoned the dahabieh again, with orders to go and wait for the travelers within sight of Luxor. And the journey by motor-caravan recommenced, between the Libyan mountains and the Bahr El-Schaguieh, which had succeeded the Bahr Yousouf. They ate lunch in Cosée, and then passed successively through Beni-Adin, Neir and Drona, situated a little to the south of the station of Siout, the ancient Lycopolis. Afterwards, there were Deir-Egch, Aboutig and Tahten, and they stopped at Idfeh, the ancient Aphroditopolis, to spend the night. Oof! Already, in this more restricted region between the river and the mountain, one sensed the proximity of the desert. At times, when the kamsin blew, whirlwinds of dust rose above the crests and fell back after far as the road the automobiles were following.

During the halt, a serious cleaning was necessary. While the bosses took a little walk in the direction of the convents, red and white specimens of Byzantine art built as much for battle as for prayer, which they contented themselves with studying from a distance, two of the drivers went to Schag, a fairly large railway station, to renew their supplies of gasoline, for no further refueling would be possible. The cook Henri and Ned accompanied them to pick up food supplies. The other servants stayed behind to guard the Duchess's vehicle, which remained there on its own, the other two having gone to fetch the supplies. Adsum, Diana, Ormus and Ahmed slowly went up toward the mountain on foot.

They made a rapid return to the camp-site when trumpets announced that the replenishment of supplies was complete. The population of the village Medinet-Atrib, a vestige of the ancient Athribis, surrounded the vehicle at a respectful distance. They were fellahs, mingled with a few Bedouins, former nomads turned cultivators. They manifested a benevolent curiosity. A little money was distributed to them; immediately, they made haste to bring fruits and flowers.

Thus night fell—beautiful night, bringing sensuality in its veils. Diana and Ormus looked at one another, with

189

the troubled thought that it might be employed more agreeably than in sleep. Momentarily, beneath the twinkling of the stars, their eyes connected—but Adsum was there. Sadly, Diana went back to her ambulant bedroom, alone.

XV. The Tedium of Abydos

Following one of the Nile's thousand petty channels, the dahabieh stopped at El-Kerbey, the village nearest to the ruins of Abydos, which enable an understanding of the vanity of human conceptions. For hundreds of centuries, that necropolis, which enclosed in its temple the mummy of Osiris, the divine founder of the Pharaonic dynasties, was the primary objective of the pilgrimage of the peoples of the Nile. Alongside Osiris and Horus, Khenti-Amenti,[23] the Sun and Death at the same time, did not represent destruction for the Egyptians, but a passage preceding immortality. Why describe its temple in a pitiful state, with its innumerable votive steles, almost razed to the ground? Why, any more, describe the temple of Ramses II, its crumbling ceilings, the great holes in its floors, and its mounds of debris?

The region is covered by small pyramids and brick mastabas. All day, Adsum, Ormus and their prisoner roamed the ruins under the guidance of the Reïs, who knew them very well. Fortunately, no bands of Cook tourists came to disturb them. Only the usual Bedouin cicerones were prowling around them, begging for the usual baksheesh. They got rid of them with a few piastres, and then ate lunch in the shadow of the temple of Site.

---

[23] Khenti-Amenti translates as "Leader of the Westerners." He was the god of Abydos, who stood guard over the necropolis, and seems to have been subsequently combined with Osiris.

After the meal, over the coffee and cigarettes, Antal Fodor said: "In the origin of this Osiris, whose legend still weighs today over the whole of Egypt, it's probable that one would discover a human individual. All these divinities, funders of religions, have a considerable fundamental similarity. A hero with nothing divine about him is the basis. Osiris chose the Sun as an emblem and a father. Subsequently, deified, he preceded the first Egyptian monarchies. Osiris came from India, the cradle of the world."

Diana addressed herself to Adsum: "Have you lived in that epoch, my Father?"

"Probably, but I have no memory of it, although I have recovered my trail in India, well before the Egyptian epoch. It's probably that the arrival of that fabulous hero on the banks of the Nile preceded the first dynasty, that of Mehnes, by many centuries, at least a millennium. The latter was able to collect the ultimate fragments of the legend and make them the foundation of a solar cult."

"Then you also believe that Osiris was a man?"

"Certainly, like Buddha, like Krishna, like the Greek Zeus, the Roman Jupiter, the Jewish Jehovah and the Christian Messiah. Only the god of Islam is all spirit and has no human form."

"Allah ill Allah!" said Ahmed.

"Yes, the unique word, which encloses everything and explains nothing."

"Amen," said the enervated Duchess. "Tomorrow, then, we leave for the Great Oasis?"

XVI. The Valley of the Kings

When the time was ripe, the vehicles having been cleaned and oiled, they departed in the evening, in order not to suffer too much from the heat. The night and the following day were spent in the sands.

The crests of the Libyan mountains had already been visible for a long time, but it was after nightfall when the motor-caravans stopped at Medinet-Habo, the village preceding the Ramesseum—the funerary temple of Ramses II. In the distance, illuminated by the moon, presently full, the two colossi of Memnon stood out in the mist rising from the Nile. Desirous of arriving at her tomb, the Pharaoh's wife directed her escort along the Fadiliveh channel, which they followed as far as the temple of Qournah. There the Reïs, ever precious, climbed into the first vehicle to guide the camel-less caravan through the mountainous maze through the middle of which wound the rocky chains on which the hypogea were built.

Finally, after some twenty-three hours, the automobiles emerged into the circular space forming the Valley of the Kings.

In the moonlight, the spectacle was quite imposing. As far as the eye could see there was nothing but steeply-hewn cliffs to the east, and steps extending westwards—which is to say, toward the desert.

That frightful massif, which is nothing but a vast necropolis, must have been formidable in prehistoric times, but the sun and the wind have gradually scoured the lamentable blocks, leaving nothing of that immense pretention but a bizarrely dislocated granitic skeleton.

The Valley of the Kings forms its approximate center, and braches extend in all directions. An imposing calm hangs over that desert of enormous stone blocks, solely troubled, from time to time, by the noise of a pebble tumbling from a summit to roll all the way down to the valley floor. Small black shadows seem to race over the ground—the shadows of countless bats, flying silently through the starry night.

Adsum, absorbed, his mind muffled, followed an uncertain mental itinerary.

"Well," said the Duchess, impatiently. "Can't you find it?"

The old man gestured to her to be silent. His eyes closed, he was seeing with his mind, hypnotizing himself in order to recover a track in the changes wrought in the mountain over three thousand years.

Finally, he started walking, going past the hypogeas where Lord Carnarvon had undertaken his excavations. A hundred meters further on, he pointed at the ground, strewn with debris.

"It's here."

Under his supervision, Ormus and Ahmed set about clearing the ground of the stones and rubble that littered it. Then, with the aid of spades, they dug down into the sand.

Adsum repeated, despotically: "Go on! It's there!"

Sitting on the footplate of the automobile, the Pharaoh's wife watched anxiously, wondering whether the two mages who had dragged her into this disagreeable pursuit might not be mad.

The depths of the excavation had already reached one and a half meters. Still nothing.

Finally, the iron head of the Reïs's spade rang on a hard flat surface. Its disengagement revealed a flat stone more than a meter square. Driving in levers and combining the efforts of their biceps, the three men—for the chauffeur had also been set to work—finally lifted up that mass and, with a superb effort, tipped it over.

A gaping hole was offered to their view.

They took a light rope-ladder from the trunk of the auto and attached it securely to the enclosing block.

Adsum went down first, with his pocket torch, whose radiance he projected ahead of him. The others, following his every movement from the top of the shaft, saw him disappear into a corridor. Air impregnated with a bituminous odor had emerged from the opening to begin with, but a current must have been established, for the sir coming up the shaft now was warm but perfectly respirable.

A considerable time went by. Finally, a little gleam reappeared, and the old mage emerged from the corridor.

"You can come down," he shouted, "but bring the headlamps from the vehicle."

"Stay here and guard the auto," said the Duchess. "We're going down alone." And, going first, she leaned into the hole, seized the rope-ladder and went down. Adsum pulled the rope from below in order to tighten it, for greater ease, but the young woman, accustomed to all manner of sports, had no need of any help.

Ormus followed her.

"There's a fissure in the mountain," said Adsum. "That's what's causing the air-flow. Go on. I've seen…go! I'll wait for you here."

The Pharaoh's wife was grateful to the old man for leaving them alone to confront those that had been themselves.

The narrow corridor was just wide enough for two people to walk abreast, very close together. They were so emotional that an inexpressible anguish gripped their throats.

The corridor was a hundred meters long, and evidently extended underneath the mountain. Suddenly, there was a right-angled turn and a rather steep downward slope. Twenty meters further on, they found themselves at the door of a tomb.

To either side, the door-posts were statues carved in the rock, and when they went inside, they saw that the statues were doubled. The two external ones were Qebehsenuef and Duamutef; the two interior ones Imsety and Hapi: the four sons of Horus the Sun; his sons, the four seasons: proof at the very entrance, that the Pharaoh had practiced the worship of Helios.

That door gave access to a rectangular room whose ceiling, in large slabs of black marble studded with golden stars, was supported by four enormous lotiform pillars, painted and gilded. Two large bands, on which were represented scenes from the life of the Pharaoh and his wife, extended around the walls, which were, like the ceiling, made of black granite constellated with golden stars.

Stone tables and gilded seats, all laden with objects of every sort: wooden, bronze and limestone statuettes, cases and trays charged with fruits and pastries reduced to dust by desiccation, weapons, garments and simulacra of every sort, for the destruction of the aliments had been foreseen and simulacra provided to replace them. An indefinable perfume was disengaged by all these venerable things. One vase looked as if it had been placed there the day before, but when Diana put out her hand to touch it, it crumbled into impalpable dust.

Holding hands, they walked toward the redoubtable location. At the back, an opening was half-masked by a bronze statue of the goddess Sekhmet, with the head of a lioness. They went around the statue and moved fearfully into the middle of the ultra-secret chamber. The double sarcophagus of the Pharaoh and his wife, on two enormous granite coffins, surged into the beams of the two headlamps. They illuminated the painted and gilded boxes enclosing the royal mummies.

Ormus leaned over the Pharaoh's tomb and raised the lid.

Tut-Ankh-Amun, his face entirely gilded, with irises of black diamond set in topaz eyes, was strangely alive, and that metalized face emitted something diabolically ironic.

Ormus, recoiling backwards, could not take his eyes off the Pharaoh, in whose yellow eyes the black diamonds seemed to animate a gaze.

Diana was also contemplating the mummy.

"And me?" she said.

Leaning over the smaller sarcophagus of the Pharaoh's wife, she too lifted the lid. An exclamation! The queen's mask was even more lifelike than that of the king. Coated with a thick layer of wax, painted and powdered, one might have thought that the young queen was asleep. Only the eyes were sunken, and the artificial irises, fallen into the depths of the orbits, glittered strangely.

Fascinated, Diana gazed at her Double, and in her emotion thought that she saw it come to life; that dead gaze drew her toward it.

Feeling that she was about to faint, she threw herself violently backwards. She would have fallen on to the stone slabs, but Ormus caught her in his arms.

He had placed the headlamp on the ground, and the glare illuminating their two silhouettes cast gigantic shadows on the ceiling.

Diana, tensed, her head tilted backwards, saw the Mage's face above her, his beautiful golden eyes plunging into her like a double jet of flame. She felt that she was skirting madness. Was it Ormus or the Pharaoh who as holding her in his arms?

In those two dormant royal mummies their other life revived, in the magnificence of youth. But no, they were other mores, other beliefs, as intransigent as the present ones: the same excesses, the same ambitions…they were human, after all! And what is five thousand years? Nothing: a moment. A second in a day, not even a century in eternity. What is five thousand years, in space and time? Nothing. Life recommences, as mysterious and as futile as before, yesterday, which is today.

Those who had been the most powerful among the powerful, and their remains, protected by the artifice of priests, and perhaps by magic, were finally about to see the light again, having not had the dispersal and the liberty of the ashes of the least of fellahs.

Those appearances, however, had had their dolors and their joys.

Hypnotized by the mummies, who had been two young and beautiful beings, Diana said aloud, replying to Ormus' thought: "I have inhabited that queen, and I have loved that Pharaoh!"

Ormus smiled. "Let's leave the past, which is still the present. We are young and beautiful. Let's love one another.

And their lips met.

They found that they were narrowly entwined, between the two granite sarcophagi.

The black marble ceiling, constellated like the night, sent the reflections of its stars down upon the two tombs, and in that indecisive light, the two mummies seemed to be laughing, while Diana swooned in the grip if the male, for which she had been waiting for such a long time.

Crazed with love, crazed with pleasure, and the satisfaction of a goal attained, after a stated gasp, crazed with sacrilege, Diana, drunk with joy, uttered a long burst of laughter, which flew and echoed through the subterranean tunnel. And for some invisible satyr,[24] it seemed that all those painted faces, the lioness Sekhmet and the four sons of Horus, joined in a chorus, and writhed.

---

[24] An oblique reference to the symbolism of Champsaur's 1924 novel *Homo deus*, subtitled *le satyre invisible* [the invisible satyr].

XVII. The Joyful Necropolis

As Ormus and Diana were united in the true tomb of Tut-Ankh-Amun, a mail-coach made a noisy entrance into the Valley of the Kings, to the clarion sound of a long trumpet blown by a white-gloved gentleman perched alongside the driver. There were twenty people inside: the flower of London fashion, touring Egypt. A few English-based foreigners were accompanying them.

First of all, there was George Manners, Duke of Rutland, and his inseparable companion William Shakespeare, both accompanied by pretty girls who had consented to leave Paris to visit the land of the mummies. They were, for the duke, the music-hall singer Marcelle Peticha, and for William Shakespeare, the Indian dancer Rana, born in Batignolles. Then there was Lord Alan Jertwery, in the company of the poet Edgard Blody, very artistic and very witty but of uncertain morals. There was Bertrand Gasllrod, a rich manufacturer from Manchester, with his niece Deborah; Oscar Plantarebourg of Rotterdam, led on a leash by a dancer who had hung up her shoes, Lise Flapy. There was also Jack Mettinons, who had just inherited an annual income of fifty thousand pounds from his father, along with a little capital, in company with three girls from the London Alhambra, whose troupe he had broken up, and a lymphatic and misanthropic old man, a multimillionaire answering to the name of Melvil Pétouard. Also to be noted were two intrepid female "globetrotters," ugly and entirely clad in tweed and leather, prudish and affected, but who gladly lingered in solitary locations with donkey-drivers and camel-drivers. The younger, who was over forty, was named Grace Edhiformotching, and the older Bell Gosie; they were both rabid feminists.

Behind the mail-coach came a truck loaded with everything necessary for a nocturnal feast among the hypogeas, organized by the agency of Thomas Cook & Son, Ltd.

In the blink of an eye, the employees had erected a large pink and white striped tent, set a table, brought out hampers of food and baskets full of bottles. "Olé! Olé!" cried Marcelle, a radiant peroxide blonde, climbing down from the coach alongside the melancholy Melvil, who was still blowing gravely into his long trumpet. She had difficulty getting down; Rutland offered her his arm and she leapt down lightly.

"So this is the Valley of the Kings?" said Rana. "From a distance, they look like public toilets."

"Horror!" cried Grace Edhiformotching. "Those are hypogea, young lady."

"Hypogea yourself!" croaked Rana. "Say, Marcelle, are you enjoying yourself here? It might be very chic to be in Egypt, in the Valley of the Kings, but I prefer Père-Lachaise."

Was Grace Edhiformotching thinking about recruiting Rana to feminism? She saw something exotic and captivating in the allure of the fake dancer. "Certainly, Miss, that Parisian cemetery is very interesting, but for you, a daughter of the sun, the hypogea are more..."

"Eh! What? Daughter of the sun? You must be loony, to tell me such tall stories!"

"I don't understand," stammered Grace. "Do you, Miss Bell?"

Miss Bell had noticed among the servants a vigorous Maltese with fiery eyes, and she turned round, rolling her eyes like a goat.

The agency guide had climbed up on a crate. "Ladies and gentlemen, the most favorable moment for visiting the hypogea at this time of year is when the moon is low enough in the sky to light the tombs full on. That will be about four o'clock in the morning."

"So we're going to be cooling our heels here waiting for the moon?" said Marcelle.

"Oh," sighed Grace Edhiformotching, "the joy and poetry of moonlight in the desert is unforgettable."

"Yes," said Bell Gosie. "A beautiful picture."

"Certainly, the moon rising in the sky is a splendid sight," said Shakespeare, "but it gives me a thirst."

He majority of the excursionists had dined too well in Luxor, and for most of them, the landscape was undulating strangely. William's appeal was very welcome, and they all precipitated into the tent set up by the employees of the Winter Palace and the Cook Agency, accustomed to these picnics in the desert. On three trestles there were four large planks and a tablecloth, surrounded by folding chairs, four torches, each one flanked by numerous candles, which made the porcelain crockery gleam and the crystal glassware sparkle. The champagne-bottles displayed their gilded necks above the ice-buckets.

It was improvised but luxurious; without giving a thought to the illustrious mummies, they emptied glasses and plates with gusto. Only the poet Edgard Blody became increasingly morose as he ate and drank.

"What can you be thinking about to pull such a long face?" cried Bertrand Gasllrod across the table. "You're not dead yet, I hope?"

"A proposition!" cried Lord Jertwery. "What if we were to shut him up in a pyramid?"

"Alas," replied the individual addressed, lugubriously, "we're like rats hurling themselves on their poison, pursuing the evil for which they're thirsty." He declaimed: "Of my cold and empty heart, I have made a ciborium of pure gold, decorated with amethyst and enamel."

"Pass me a bit!" cried Rana. "I'll gobble you up, man with a heart of gold!"

"Georgie, Georgie!" called Marcelle Peticha. "Come and sit with me, and leave Mettinons to his girls."

"Marcelle, you'll never guess the proposition that Mettinons has just put to me."

"It can only be a dishonest one."

"He's offered to swap me his three girls for Marcelle Peticha."

"Three angels for one demon? You'd lose on the deal, my lad."

Shakespeare got to his feet. "Savor these aphorisms, all of you. One: women are angels, so long as one doesn't possess them. Two: the soul of happiness expires in enjoyment. Three: No one has ever found love satisfied as sweet as desire on its knees. Four: Possession makes masters, resistance beggars. Friends, meditate on all that…and pour me a drink!"

"William, I'll make you a cuckold if your slander women—pig!"

"No," Shakespeare replied. "I don't care—and that, brown Rana, takes all the pleasure out of deception."

"Gentlemen," said Lise Flapy, emptying her glass, I'll offer my favors almost gratis to anyone who can say make Master Plantarebourg of Rotterdam, here present, say something witty."

Oscar laughed loudly, but without proffering a word.

"I accept," said Gasllrod. "Go on, Deborah, Go on, niece!"

Deborah was a magnificent Jewess, with jet-black eyes and hair. Without raising an eyebrow, she went to pick up a champagne-bucket from which four bottles were sticking out, and went to sit down facing Plantarebourg. The Dutchman laughed even louder, but did not say a word. The impassive Jewess popped the cork of one bottle and set it down in front of him. Then, uncorking a second, she clinked the two together. "Bottoms up!" she said—and, tipping her head back, she drank straight from the bottle. Plantarebourg did the same, but with less avidity.

Deborah uncorked the other two bottles.

"Bottoms up!"

The Dutchman drank, but went as red as a brick.

"Bring some more bottles," said the Jewess.

"He'll drink, but he'll stay mute!" cried Lidde.

"Bottoms up!" said Deborah.

"Bravo!" said Shakespeare. "There's a mettlesome lass!"

"She's my niece," said Bertrand, proudly.

"*Gott ver drin!*" groaned the Dutchman. "I'm drowning."

"He spoke!" howled the company.

"That's true, but it wasn't very witty."

"Bottoms up!"

The Dutchman got up, hanging on to the table.

"I'll speak," he said. "Even if I have to lie, I'll speak. Yes, Bertrand, your niece is the most beautiful, and anyone who says otherwise is a fool. That frog takes me for an imbecile because I prefer to stay silent rather than reply to her silly prattle. Uncle Bertrand, your niece is a pearl, a diamond. Give her to me! I'll marry her!"

"Bravo!" cried the choir. "Hurrah for Deborah and Bertrand!"

Why did that scene, instead of cheering the poet up, put the lid on his sadness? Edgard dissolved in tears.

"Deborah!" called Bertrand.

The beautiful Jewess uncorked a bottle and looked at her uncle. The latter pointed to the deplorable rhymer. "Console that poor soul."

The Jewess got up, went to the despairing man and, picking him up under her arm, sat him down on her knee. Edgard embraced her recklessly and inundated her with tears. Tranquilly, Deborah seized a napkin, wiped the lamentable visage, then grabbed a bottle and put the neck between his teeth. "Go on, down the hatch!" she said.

General hilarity.

"That one's a hoot!" cried Rana, ecstatically. "She's not a woman, she's a sponge."

"She's my niece," said Bertrand again, proudly.

"Oo la la!" said Marcelle Peticha. "I've got a tummy-ache. Rub me, Georgie!"

There was an extraordinary animation under the tent. Rutland massaged Marcelle Peticha, who, tickled, waved her arms and legs. Jack Mettinons made his three girls dance, and Miss Bell, disdaining Grace's conversation, gave the handsome Maltese a nudge every time his duties as a waiter brought him within range.

At that moment, an automobile horn resounded in the valley, and a superb limousine stopped in front of the excursionists' tent. Three men got down and came inside.

"Milords and ladies," said the one who appeared to be the master, "I have the honor of saluting you."

The Duke of Rutland got to his feet. "What! Your Majesty deigns..."

"Leave my majesty out of it, my dear Rutland. I know that wherever you are, it's never boring, and my word, I'll permit myself to join you. Sit down, I beg you, and make room for me at our table."

At the title "Majesty" everyone had got up, striving to strike a correct attitude—even Deborah, who, having put the poet down, straightened up while the Duke of Rutland made the introduction.

"His Majesty Fuad I, our venerated King of Egypt."

The king started laughing. "No, Rutland, anything else you wish, but no veneration—and allow me to explain my presence here, Gentlemen. While you are digging up the tombs of my ancestors, I'm striving, as the reigning Pharaoh, to draw the natural resources from beneath the ground of my old Egypt—which, I hope, will be as prodigious as its surface. Accompanied by these gentlemen, I'm prospecting my kingdom, in order to extract a return from it, more prosaic than that of thousand-year-old mummies, but adapted to our epoch. I, Gentlemen, care little about my Double, and I beg you to believe that I shall build no pyramids. Do you think I'm in the right, pretty lady?"

He was addressing Marcelle Peticha.

Very proud of having attracted the attention of a king, the actress shot him an incendiary gaze with her lovely eyes. "Of course you're right, Sire…Majesty."

Rutland gave Marcelle a warning dig in the ribs.

"Pardon, Sire—I don't know the protocol."

"I prefer it, Mademoiselle. Besides which, I'm traveling incognito. Call me Ismael—Ismael Pasha."

"Chic! I like that better. Well, Mr. Ismael Pasha, to our health!"

"Thank you, Mademoiselle..."

"Marcelle Peticha, of the theaters of Paris."

"Mademoiselle Peticha, I have applauded you in a charming operetta by François Berlu, *Cupidon*."[25]

And the conversation took a semi-artistic, semi-gallant turn, continued between Fuad I and the pretty singer. Very much in the swing of things, the modern successor of the Pharaohs was not at all avid to assume the rank of crowned head. As gallant as Henri IV and François I, having studied in Paris, he had retained happy memories of his youth, and the charming king was doing his best to prolong it—which did not prevent him envisaging means to make the soil of his country yield mineral treasures forgotten to date. In the company of two engineers, he was traveling his domain, having already discovered some significant deposits, and the search promised to be very rewarding. The intelligent monarch did not consider himself to be following the path imposed by Providence with regard to his people, and reckoned that Egypt would be neither better nor worse off without him.

"What a good idea, my dear Duke," said the king to Rutland, "to come and visit my ancestors with these young ladies. It will permit me to prove to them that not all Egyptians are mummified."

"And yet I, personally, have come here to see a mummy: my wife's."

"But I met the Duchess a little while ago, and there was nothing of the mummy about her."

---

[25] A fictitious citation; "*avoir la berlue*" means to suffer from delusions.

"It's a strange story. Can you imagine, Sire, that for some years the Duchess has devoted herself ardently to the mysteries of the afterlife?"

"Lady Rutland seems to me to be too young and too beautiful to cloud her brain with such abstract ideas. I thought occultism was reserved for somewhat mature ladies on the decline, like, for example, the late Duchesse de Pomar.[26] She believed that she had been Mary Queen of Scots in one of her previous incarnations."

"Well, for my wife, it's the wife of Tut-Ankh-Amun that she imagines herself to have been: a Pharaoh's wife."

Fuad I burst out laughing. "Oh, what a joke…!"

"That's also my opinion, Sire. But I must say, in my wife's defense, that she's been aided to find a whole series of avatars by two adventurers of premier quality."

The King of Egypt, in his high-waisted suit, baggy in front, light brown shoes and motoring helmet, smiled in a fashion that said a lot. "And, as a good husband incapable of contradicting a lovely woman, you've abandoned her to her mania. Completely liberated, you can lead a joyous life, and bring the fine feminine flower of Parisian life to us here, in the desert."

Marcelle strove to blush with modesty, and bowed. "Oh, Majesty! Your Majesty is too indulgent."

"Not Majesty, my beautiful child, Ismael—simply Ismael." Don't you like that name? You see, Mademoiselle, it's agreeable to me that the Europeans bring us,

---

[26] Maria de Mariategui, Lady Caithness, Duchesse de Medina Pomar (1830-1895) was an occultist and spiritualist who spent much of her time in Paris, although theoretically resident in England with her Scottish husband.

who are blasé with regard antique beauty, a pretty Parisian face. The defunct Pharaohs are vindictive; they punish the indiscreet persons who come to disturb their sleep. The ancient Egyptians, in building these hypogea, took infinite care to hide their final retreat, but they only succeeded in attracting thieves." The king stood up. "I'm subject to the influence of these illustrious mummies, and I feel a trifle stiff. If you wish, Mademoiselle, it would give me pleasure to take stroll in your company."

Marcelle got up swiftly, ready to follow him.

"With your permission, my dear Duke..." the King said to Rutland, for form's sake.

The Duke had an equivocal smile, but what could he do except bow to the King's desire? So he bowed, respectfully, while the sovereign linked arms with the young actress and led her away.

The time to visit the hypogea had arrived. The Agency guide came to make the announcement.

Slightly excited by the champagne, everyone got up, with varying degrees of difficulty, tottering slightly, and then set out in quest of their binoculars, Kodaks and other items with which a self-respecting excursionist takes care to equip himself. The servants picked up candles and electric torches, and the troop set off, in good enough order, toward he tombs of the Pharaohs.

Rutland, slightly vexed at seeing his conquest stolen, and not feeling any desire to visit the mummies without his pretty actress, had sat down again, and lit a cigar. As Shakespeare has little desire to zigzag through sand and rubble, he also took advantage of the opportunity to rest. He confided Rana to the inoffensive old misogynist and, collecting the few bottles that remained on the table, sat down facing his friend.

XVIII. The Lucky Find

On emerging from the tent His Egyptian Majesty, who had no interest in visiting the hypogea, drew his companion through the high hills along the cliff where the tombs were hollowed out. While flirting with the young woman, and taking a few preliminary liberties, the monarch scrutinized the mountain with his gaze in search of a suitable niche. The sand offered a sufficiently soft bed, but it was terribly enameled with stones fallen from the millenarian funereal ruins.

Marcelle Peticha, meanwhile, found the adventure as amusing as possible and even more flattering.

The King, for his part was frankly happy; he was about to possess an alluring and pretty hyperblonde, sparkling with pert Parisian spirit, with the chic that the word "Parisian" comprises for foreigners. Then again, it amused him to put one over on an Englishman. It is always a trifle vexing to be a protégé, not to be one's own master, and the unfortunate Duke of Rutland could take a joke.

While idling and chatting the lovers had covered a good deal of ground. A rocky mass protruded vertically from the sand, seemingly promising the couple the shelter they sought; they went around the hillock and were surprised to discover a superb automobile, momentarily abandoned.

"I'll requisition it," said Ismael Pasha.

How had the Duchess of Rutland's motor-caravan, entrusted to the care of Ahmed and the driver, come to be abandoned?

Life is beautiful, even for kings!

XIX. Drunken Speech

Left alone at the deserted table, Rutland and Shakespeare pursued their own trains of thought, semi-drunk, pouring out the excess of their confused ideas, a trifle overexcited by too-oft-repeated libations.

"To the Devil with all women!" hiccupped the Duke. "It only takes some fellow with any sort of notoriety to pass by for them to fling their arms around his neck. I couldn't care less about that chit of an actress, but to leave me—who maintains her in a chic enough fashion—for a petty king, a fellow who, but for England, wouldn't be able to stand up! That sickens me, Will; that positively sickens me, old man."

"Have a drink. Nothing better to quell the bile. All that, you see, is a question of feminine vanity. One doesn't sleep with a king every day—and then, put yourself in her place. Suppose a queen tipped you the wink... It's necessary, you see, to take life for what it's worth, and, with a little imagination, take the birds for musicians, the sand you're treading on for a drawing-room carpet, flowers for lovely ladies, and your staggering steps for the latest dance-craze. Chagrin has less purchase on the individual when he snaps his fingers at it and treats it lightly."

"You can talk, William, you can talk! I can feel myself becoming neurasthenic, splenetic, anything you like. I'm annoyed; I see everything in black."

"Because you're not drunk enough! Look at me—I'm fifty years old and I'm younger than you. Why? Because I've never believed that it would happen. Don't imagine for that that I love life. One can't love the incomprehensible, but death frightens me even more. The most difficult, most repulsive life—destitution, illness, old age, even prison—is a paradise compared with what we dread of death!"

"Yes," Rutland rehiccuped. "To die! And to go we don't know where. To be lying between two cold partitions and thinking! This sensitive body, full of warmth and movement, must become a noxious mud, while the mind, launched into the immensity of the Universe, will wander like a vagabond...more wretched than the most wretched...if it wanders alone..."

"My God! That's the theory of the Mage Ormus coming back to your mind. Then again, what does it matter to you to be cuckolded today by a true descendant of the Pharaohs, when your wife's doing likewise with a fake Pharaoh, an adventurer, a sorcerer—not that proper, in sum. But he has an allure, the swine, and you don't look like much beside him, William!"

"Why are you calling me William? I'm a cuckold but not a William. Pour me a drink!"

"I thought I'd do you the honor, because, for my part, I'm damned if I'd want to be Rutland."

"Master Shakespeare," said the Duke, in a dignified manner, "I believe you're lacking in respect for the man who feeds you."

"Is that a reproach, Milord? So be it! One humiliates a friend of twenty years; one reproaches him for a morsel of bread. Pride, there is thy sting! That's all right—I'm going; I'm leaving you and going back to the desert." He broke into song: "In search of li-ber-tee!" He tried to get up, but fell back on to his chair, heavily. "That's chagrin," he muttered. "It's dolor that's overwhelming me."

The Duke dissolved in tears. "Then you're leaving me too? Everyone's abandoning me. Poor me!"

"Come on, don't cry," said Shakespeare, compassionately. "Don't cry—you'll dry yourself out, and it's already dry enough here. By Jove, I'm thirsty! What possessed you to bring us to this accursed place?"

Rutland was momentarily nonplussed. "Here? To begin with, where are we?"

"You've totally lost it, then? But look, we're in Egypt—the land of the mummies."

"Mummies? Pour me a drink, Will—mummies? Yes, of course—we're here to see my wife's mummy."

"What? That poor Duchess has been mummified? Not surprising, after all, in dry America."

"William, this can't go on any longer. I need to get my wife back."

"I approve. It's your husbandly duty. But if she's a mummy…?

"Exactly—nothing to be done. Are you coming?"

"Where?"

"To see my wife's mummy."

"Do you know where it is?"

"Come on, I tell you. My heart will guide me."

"*Marchons! Marchons!*—as in that French hymn, the *Marseillaise*. But aren't you thirsty?"

"Of course—only, there aren't any more bottles."

"Old chap, one can't embark like that in machines…tombs…without taking a few bottles. Let's search."

Supporting one another, they made a tour of the table.

"Saved!" said Rutland. "Look over there."

On the ground, next to the canvas, there was one more basket, half-full.

"Hurrah! Let's put two bottles in our pockets, and forward ho!"

Arm in arm, lurching, they went out. Behind the supply-truck they could hear the Agency staff making merry with the remains of the feast. Everything around the tent was calm and silent. A few hundred meters away, along the almost-sheer rock-face in which the hypogea were hollowed out, a dark group was agitating: the excursionists and their guide.

Rutland made a disdainful gesture. "There are no mummies in there that Lord Carnarvon didn't find. Let's search further on."

"Let's search!" babbled Shakespeare, walking drowsily and singing, thickly: "Let's search...let's...search...!"

XX. Fogs and Zigzags

They had gone into the maze of the valley, and were bumping into debris, but with a champagnesque obstinacy, Rutland dragged his companion along. Far from dissipating their drunkenness, the cool night air augmented it—or at least, if their step was slightly more assured, there was nothing but fumes in their brains.

"Hey!" said the Duke, suddenly. "What's that?"

A few meters away there was a hole in the ground, from which light was emerging. Hazard had brought the two companions to the shaft of the tomb of Tut-Ankh-Amun. The two friends drew nearer, on tiptoe. The gleam was coming from a tunnel whose entrance was perceptible at the bottom of the shaft.

"There's a ladder," said the Duke. "I'll go first."

Adroitly enough, he introduced himself into the hole and took hold of the ladder he had glimpsed.

"Brrrr!" he said. "It's spinning." Nevertheless, clinging on, he let himself slide down.

"Dirty business!" Shakespeare muttered. "I'll never get down there myself."

He looked into the depths of the shaft and saw George, who was beckoning to his friend with an air of mystery.

Curiosity got the better of prudence, and Shakespeare introduced himself into the orifice in his turn, almost filling it, and searched for the ladder with his foot. He did not encounter anything, and remained suspended by his hands from the rim of the shaft. He was too heavy, though, and was forced to let go and fall into the void. Fortunately, his extended arms encountered the

215

rope-ladder and he clung on, with an energy multiplied tenfold by fear. He spun momentarily, and then regained his aplomb, one of his feet having found a rung, and he descended—or, more precisely, lowered himself down—to the bottom.

"Shh, Will!" said Lord Rutland. "Keep quiet, and come this way."

He dragged Shakespeare along, and they both advanced into the tunnel. On the ground there was an automobile headlamp, which was emitting a dazzling light. A little further on, at a bend in the tunnel, sheltered from the overly bright light, was a dark mass surmounted by a head of white hair. A long beard descended in a cascade over the sleeper's breast—for Adsum had fallen asleep while waiting for Ormus and Diana.

"Saint Peter at the entrance to Paradise," said William.

"Let's not wake him. He might be the Devil in disguise."

With ridiculously excessive precautions, the two innocents went past the old man, without recognizing him, sticking their tongues out at him and pulling faces. Adsum was far from their thoughts at present.

Rutland, who had picked up the headlamp, went on ahead. With difficulty, they went down the steep corridor, whose narrowness permitted them to support themselves on its side walls.

XXI. Shakespearean Vaudeville

The lovers had forgotten the time and the place. Dozing in one another's arms, they were lying on the fine sand that covered the floor of the mortuary cavern. The headlamp, set down on the floor beside the sarcophagus, illuminated one side of the room vividly, and on the wall at that exact spot, was a double-banded fresco representing the marriage of Tut-Ankh-Amun, in which, sitting on a double throne wearing tall tiaras, the sovereigns were watching a procession of functionaries and priests, bringing their good wishes and offerings to the two royal divinities.

Opening his eyes, Ormus cocked an ear toward the door. Strange noises were coming from the corridor.

Gently disengaging himself from the Duchess's arm, which was around his neck, he got up and headed toward the stir. In the distance, at the far end of the long tunnel, two men were advancing awkwardly, holding on to the walls. One of them was projecting the light of an automobile headlamp that he was holding.

Have we been in the cave that long? Ormus wondered. *Adsum's doubtless become impatient. I have to wake Diana, to go back.*

He heard the sound of a heavy fall, accompanied by an oath: "My God! Help me, George, I slipped!"

The man carrying the headlamp turned back to help the other to his feet. As he set his lantern down, his face appeared in the light.

The Duke of Rutland and Shakespeare! Ormus said to himself. *That's extraordinary! How did they get here?*

Swiftly, he went back, awoke the Duchess with a kiss, and told her about her husband's approach—which made the young woman burst out laughing

"As good ideas go, this isn't one of his best!"

Slowly and painfully, the two friends finally reached the door of the tomb.

"I told you that my heart would guide me. My wife is here, I swear."

"Yes, but hang on a minute. I'm dying of thirst. That diabolical corridor had a terrible slope—no means of stopping to drink a drop."

"It's very warm here. We haven't been very clever. We should have brought Saint Peter. He lives down here—he must have a good cellar. I'll go look for him."

"Stay, George. You'll break your neck going back down. And first, you'd have to climb back up."

That reasoning convinced Rutland. They went into the vestibule and looked around in astonishment. After a moment spent trying to bring a little order into their ides, they renounced the attempt and, sitting down on the pedestals of the statues in the doorway, they broke the neck of a bottle and took long draughts. This time, their thirst was justified, for the staggering walk through the corridors, whose millennial dust they had awkwardly kicked up, had dried out their throats.

"Ah, that's better!" said William, finally, throwing away the empty bottle. "Now take me to present my respects to Lady Rutland."

"It must be that way," said the Duke, pointing to the mortuary chamber. "This, my dear chap, is only the antechamber."

"Tortuous, these old boys," said Shakespeare. "A chap really shouldn't go to so much trouble to wrap up his old carcass."

They went into the chamber. Their last libation had finished them off; nothing could any longer astonish them. They headed for the sarcophagi and raised the lantern over the Pharaoh's tomb."

"It's really him!" exclaimed Rutland. "Do you recognize the mage Ormus? Look. Look, he's laughing—he doesn't give a damn about me, of course. Dirty swine!"

"And here's your wife," added Shakespeare. "As a resemblance, it could be better—but it's her, all the same." He bowed respectfully. "Your humble servant, Milady."

"Alas, my poor Diana!" stammered the Duke, tearfully. "You remember her, Will—she was a woman of infinite jest, of most excellent fancy, and now she causes me an unimaginable horror. And to think that here are those lips that I've kissed, this lovely body that I've..."

"Sacrilege!" clamored a thunderous voice, which vibrated like a gong in the cage of stone. "Sacrilege! What are you doing here?"

The two profaners turned round. On the threshold of the tomb, two specters were looking at them: the Pharaoh and his wife were barring their way.

The Duke, terrified, dropped the headlamp, which broke and went out. A double burst of laughter vibrated in the gloom.

Bewildered, the two drunks groped their way through the darkness. Shakespeare bumped in to the lids thrown on to the floor, and fell; his head slammed into the wall and he lost consciousness.

"William!" called the Duke, in a tremulous voice. "Answer me, William! Where are you?"

Deathly silence.

Rutland raised his hands to his forehead, which was bursting. His drunkenness had dissipated under the shock of fear, as if by enchantment, and he thought he was going mad. It suddenly seemed to him that a blue light had invaded the room, and an acrid odor seized his throat.

He launched himself in the direction that appeared to him to be that of the door, cannoned into the sarcophagus of the Pharaoh's wife on the way, and, not finding anything to grab on to, stumbled and fell into the coffin, smashing the mummy as he fell.

A fine dust rose up, covering him with impalpable ash. That was the last straw! He moaned feebly and lost consciousness, while Shakespeare, recovering from his own faint, sang, unthinkingly:

"If the dead are crazy, I'm alive and crazy...if the dead are drunk..."

XXII. Explanations

This, quite simply, is what had happened: Diana and Ormus had picked up the two lids covering the mummies and had hidden behind them to either side of the door. They had thus witnessed the burlesque entrance of the two friends, and their reflections. Things might have taken an embarrassing turn for the Duchess if the Mage had not interrupted them with his thunderous invective: "Sacrilege! Sacrilege!"

On seeing the two painted lids standing in front of the door, the drunkards had been deluded, and in his fright, the Duke had dropped the lantern, which had broken. Throwing down the two lids, Diana and Fodor had fled, leaving the intruders to recover from their confusion as best they could.

One of the lids had fallen on top of the lantern, covering the debris; the wick, not quite extinct, had ignited the spilled gasoline and set fire to the extremely dry lid—hence the blue light that had frightened the Duke so much and the suffocating odor that had invaded the little mortuary chamber.

The lid continued to burn—slowly and flamelessly, fortunately for the two victims of their untimely curiosity. The airflow drew the smoke into the corridor and from the corridor to the world outside, beneath the impassive stars.

XXIII. Lovers, Prehistoric and Modern

Laughing like lunatics and lovers, Ormus and Diana went back to Adsum. They found him at the bottom of the shaft, and their laughter resumed, more heartily.

"The sight of your mummies, your Doubles, has put you in a merry mood, my children. I confess, to my shame, that the great silence reigning here carried me off into sleep. When I woke up, I found myself in darkness; I was groping around for my lantern and getting ready to go back up."

"Then you haven't seen anyone in the hypogeum?"

"No. Has someone come in while I was asleep?"

"Yes—and you'll laugh like us when you know who. Let's get out first."

When all three of them were outside, the old savant said: "Push back the stone that seals the shaft."

"Oh no!" said Diana, swiftly. "They've been punished enough. We can't do that."

And in a few words, they explained to the old mage what had happened in the tomb—not all of it, however; merely the final act.

"Strictly speaking," Ormus concluded, "we might get the Duke back up, if he hasn't gone mad. As for Shakespeare, we'd need reinforcements for that obesity. Stay here, Father—we'll go look for Ahmed and the chauffeur, and we'll come back.

Like two schoolchildren on vacation, the two lovers drew away.

Adsum watched them go, pensively...

XXIV. The King Amuses Himself

They found their automobile where they had left it, but its guardians had disappeared.

"Where are they?" said the Duchess. "This isn't the kind of place to go for a stroll, though."

A burst of high-pitched laughter resounded in the vehicle.

"That's too much!" cried Diana. "They're inside with a woman, making mock of us."

Ormus seized the handle brutally and opened the door. What he saw nailed him to the spot.

There was an agitation inside, and then a man leapt lightly on to the sand. He made a slight gesture of surprise on recognizing the Duchess of Rutland.

"Truly, Madame, I'm favored by the gods. By what fortunate hazard do I have the joy of meeting you again?"

The Duchess and the Mage had immediately recognized the sovereign of the two Egypts.

"I see, Sire, that after having given you passage in my dahabieh, you're now honoring my motor-caravan with your presence."

"While out walking with a friend, I took the liberty, in the absence of the owners, of taking a look at its interior decoration."

"Sire, a king in his kingdom is at home everywhere."

The king bowed gallantly. During this conversation, young Marcelle had readjusted her clothing. She showed her pretty face in the doorway.

"Come out, Mademoiselle, so that I can introduce you to our hostess." He turned to the Duchess. "Marcelle Peticha, the blondest star of the Parisian theaters."

"I've had the pleasure of applauding Mademoiselle, and I hope she will retain a pleasant memory of my hospitality."

The delightful peroxide blonde judged it her duty to enter into conversation with the Duchess. "On a Cook excursion, with my friend the Duke of Rutland..." In response to the signals that the king was making, she stopped short, nonplussed.

Softly, Diana said to Ormus: "Cuckolded twice on the same day, then? That's a record!"

As if to provide a salutary diversion, Ahmed and the chauffeur suddenly appeared.

"Well," said the Duchess, "where have you been? Is this how you guard my vehicle?"

The Reïs started to explain, but the Duchess cut him off: "No need! Will you excuse me, Sire?"

The king moved away, chatting to Antal Fodor.

"Let's hurry, then," said Ahmed, after having listened to Diana's explanations. The two unfortunates might have died of fright. There's a rope in the trunk; I'll bring it along. In the meantime, try to get rid of the King."

"My car is over there," His Majesty said to Ormus. "I'm on a prospecting expedition with two of my engineers...that seems to surprise you. You don't suppose that I've come here to dig up my ancestors, as my good friends the English are doing? No, Egypt possesses a subsoil as rich in naphtha as in archeological relics. I'm a living and practical Pharaoh. If, one day, I feel the steps of my throne cracking, I'll seek refuge in Paris; it's necessary not to arrive there with empty pockets."

Antal Fodor, the occultist arriviste, thought him the antithesis of the Pharaohs who represented ancient Egypt, feeling no repulsion at the idea of becoming an oil-merchant. And to whom was he recounting his project? To one of those millenarian Pharaohs, alive!

The monarch consulted his wristwatch. "Time's passing too quickly. May I say goodbye to the Duchess of Rutland?" He advanced toward her and kissed her hand. Then he pointed to the Cook Agency encampment, whose tent could be seen from far away, luminously white in the moonlight.

"I need to take Mademoiselle back."

The actress was wearing a ring on her finger, set with a magnificent emerald carved into the form of a scarab—perhaps a souvenir.

In an unceremoniously comradely fashion, the King held his hand out to Ormus, who bowed to him.

XXV. The Resurrection

A few minutes later, Diana, Adsum, Ormus, Ahmed and the chauffeur were standing beside the opening of the tomb of Tut-Ankh-Amun. While the three rescuers went down, the Duchess told the Father about the royal incident.

Scarcely were Ormus and his two companions in the long narrow corridor leading to the mortuary chamber than an odor of smoke caught them in the throat. As it was tolerable, though, they went on. At the far end they saw Shakespeare, who was snoring, his head resting on a granite statue of Thoth that had been knocked over in the chaos.

"He's snoring, so he's not dead, just drunk," said Ahmed. "Let's hope that the other's in the same fortunate condition."

There was no one in the funerary chamber, however, where the charred lid was quietly finishing its consumption. The chauffeur lifted his lantern above the sarcophagus. The Pharaoh in the golden mask was still smiling enigmatically. In the other sarcophagus, the collapsed Duke was no longer showing any sign of life. Ormus and Ahmed lifted Rutland out, and the Mage applied his ear anxiously to the unconscious man's breast.

"Good—there's still time," he said to the two men, standing up. He took a small pen-knife from his pocket and opened a vein in the left arm. At first the blood ran black and thick, and then more brightly.

"He'll pull through," the Mage continued. "The man's drunk, and fear caused him to suffer a cerebral congestion. It's serious. We need to get him out of here in a hurry."

The two men carried Rutland while Ormus lit their path. When they reached the shaft Ahmed attached the body to his back and, taking hold of the rope, completed the climb in two minutes. Up above, Diana and Adsum detached the sick man, and while they took care of him, the Reïs let himself down again.

When he got back to Shakespeare he shook him rudely.

"Damn!" groaned the drunk. "I'm dead and buried, leave me alone—or give me something to drink. It's devilishly hot in this sub-branch of Hell."

Swiveling his eyes around him, he recognized Ormus.

"What! The sorcerer's here? Henchman of the Devil, have you come on your master's behalf to look for old Will? That's all right—I'll go with you. But give me a drink first."

"If you want a drink, Master Will, you'll have to get out of here first, and back into the daylight. Your friend Rutland's waiting for you."

Shakespeare rubbed his head energetically. "Alas, poor Yorick! This pillow is terribly hard. So George is waiting for me. What are we doing today?"

"Look where you are, Master Will, and try to remember."

The fat man followed this advice, while Ormus paraded the light of the headlamp around. Vaguely, he remembered, but in his confused mind, the events had no more value for him than a dream. On seeing the place where he was, he thought that he really was dreaming, and lay down again, passing his hands over his forehead as if to drive away the evil images.

"What a nightmare! It's stupid, stupid!"

"Come on, get up," said Ormus, "or I'll leave you in the tomb."

The word "tomb" made the drunkard sit up. "What? It's not a dream, then—it's serious."

"Very serious. It's dangerous for you to stay here any longer. Come quickly!"

"If the hour of danger has come, then it isn't still to come. There's a Providence predestined for the death of a sparrow. Why shouldn't there be one for the death of William Shakespeare?"

Bustled somewhat by Ahmed and the chauffeur, the drunkard succeeded in standing up, but he continued to follow his train of thought. "And don't go thinking that I'm drunk."

The two men grabbed him by the arms and dragged him away. While lighting the way, Ormus lent a hand in shivering the obstinate drunk, who continued his monologue.

"Truly, is a little champagne sufficient to celebrate the glory that our most transcendent exploits merit? Drunkenness, in spite of itself, topples the edifice of reason, is the leaven of the most praiseworthy qualities."

Carried, pulled and pushed, William arrived as best he could at the bottom of the shaft. Strong as Ahmed was, he could not think of carrying the fat man up on his back. A rope was looped under his arms; then the three men climbed up. Bracing themselves with the rope, they tried to hoist their cumbersome burden up.

Feeling himself lifted from the ground, William started howling: "Aiee! Aiee! Are you trying to cut me in two?"

But the three men renounced their rescue attempt and let the fat man fall back.

"He isn't helping us at all," said the Reïs. "We'll never get him up with the rope. What can we do?" After a pause, he shouted: "Hey—use the ladder, Mr. Shakespeare. We'll support you."

"Me. climb up that thread? You're mad—completely crazy. Leave me be and send me down a few bottles to keep me company. Send my Juliet, too, we'll sing like caged birds. Thus, we'll spend our lives, singing and telling old tales, laughing, in the gilded blue land that haunts the brain of Romeo…no, rum without water…"

"He's completely out of his mind," said the Reïs. "I can only see one way of getting him out of here. Bring the auto, tie the rope to it, and set it going. The poet will come up very gently."

"Let's try," said Ormus.

It was, however, impossible to get the vehicle to the orifice of the shaft. They pulled out the ladder and ted it to the end of the rope.

During these preparations, the bee in Shakespeare's bonnet had turned another somersault. From the bottom of his hole, he howled: "Furious winds! Blow to burst your cheeks! Cataracts and hurricanes, disgorge yourselves and drown these imbecile pyramids! Sulfurous lightning, as rapid as thoughts, harbinger of the thunderbolt that cleaves oaks, come to me! And you, exterminating thunder! Aiee! Aiee! It's death!"

Abruptly tugged by the auto, set in motion, the rope lifted him up, not at all gently, and Shakespeare spun as he rose rapidly.

"Stop!" cried Ahmed, as the terrified head of the package arrived at the rim.

The poor fellow was no more than a lamentable wreck, incapable of attempting a movement. Once he was in the light he opened an eye.

"Since I've been a man," he said, "I can't remember having lived through such a night..."

"And here's the dawn," said Adsum. "My children, it's necessary to hurry if we don't want anyone to discover your Doubles' true sepulcher."

All putting themselves to the task, they replaced the stone over the orifice of the shaft and erased the traces of their passage. In the meantime, the Duchess lavished cares upon he Duke, who was breathing more easily but was still unconscious.

Rapidly refreshed by the pure air, William said: "Finally, Milady, I find you again in the flesh, and in beauty. I prefer that."

"What do you mean, Master Will? It ought to be me who's astonished to meet you in Egypt, more in the flesh than ever."

The parasite with rich eyes but poor hands mastered his wonderstruck face.

"Am I or am I not? That's the question that I'm asking. Your presence proves that I am. Never have I had so much joy in contemplating your lovely face, Milady. I was struggling between dream and reality, and George wasn't there to prove to me that it wasn't a dream."

"Why has your friend pursued me all the way here? He shouldn't have done that."

Duchess, my homonym said; 'That woman that cannot make her fault her husband's occasion, let her never nurse her child herself, for she will breed it like a fool!'[27] Patience—life is short!"

---

[27] *As You Like It*, Act IV, scene 1.

"William, I know your affection for the Duke. Watch over him when he recovers his senses. He needs care. I know you won't fail him. And you, Reïs, stay with these gentlemen. Take the invalid to my hotel in Abydos in my personal motor-caravan. Lie him down in my bed. I give you full confidence, Ahmed, and full credit."

For his part, Shakespeare made no reply. He had bowed his head as a sign of assent. He gazed at his friend, and two heavy tears—the only ones he had ever shed—rolled down his cheeks.

XXVI. The Dawn of Love

The night, so fecund in events, had come to an end. Over the Arabian mountains, the sun rose resplendently and its rays caressed the Nile, reduced at that time of the year to the breadth of its bed; it would not be for another month that the first rush of benevolent waves would reach Thebes. Thanks to the barrage, the river remains navigable all year round, and the river-dwellers await without impatience the flood whose regularly-distributed waters fecundate the whole of Egypt.

The rise of the day star had a grandiose aspect. The air of Egypt, admirable in its purity and almost completely devoid of water vapor, does not filter the light as in Europe; it as an abrupt and radiant eruption of the sun above the horizon; Horus, as soon as he is risen, shines with a glittering glare, a cascade of fire that surges from the mountains, pouring over the Delta and inundating the sands of the Libyan desert, the limpid waves of which climb into the sky in the distance.

It as in the full light of dawn, therefore, the dazzle of the young morning, that the Duchess's automobile retraced the route it had followed the previous evening in the moonlight. The roadster hired to replace the motor-caravan that was carrying the Duke of Rutland, Shakespeare and the Reïs to Abydos, had four seats. Adsum was next to the driver; Diana and Ormus were installed in the rear.

The lovers abandoned themselves to the charm of that glorious morning, full of azure, sunlight and delight for them. The Duchess was like a beautiful rose displaying all the splendor of its bloom; her eyes were shining with a voluptuous gleam, her lips were redder and her complexion more animated. As for Ormus, his triumphant youth had got the upper hand over the austere reserve of the Mage, and he was no longer anything but a victorious lover.

The travelers were silent, savoring the joy of the moment; the lovers were holding hands, and their silence seemed to be populated with kisses.

The old Mage was pensive. His intuition had told him what had happened, and sadness overcame him at the thought that the goal that he had sought for so long would doubtless never be attained. But how could he impede the call of life, of love, between two young people, beautiful and full of health? Destiny is the master, and what can our poor terrestrial desires do against invisible and omnipotent forces? In his Oriental fatalism, Adsum repeated an old Arab proverb: "No one can obtain the fate that is not written for him, and what is written, none can avoid."

"Happy, Diana, my darling?" asked Ormus, softly.

"Very happy, my love. I was asleep, and you have woken me up, and revealed me to myself. Why didn't you come into my life sooner?"

"I came when I heard your call."

"What do you mean?"

"We have already belonged to one either in the course of the ages, as you know. Diana, for me you are what is known as 'the duality,' my complementary soul, the other half of my divided being, the one who was and always will be mine through successive incarnations, because she reestablishes the unity of our original self. All the people on Earth have their dualities, for which they search unconsciously, without ever encountering them. That is what explains infidelities and abandonments, which are simply the disappointments of an unrealized ideal, the fleeting glimmer mistaken for the pure flame of love. This time, once again, the superior forces have permitted us to meet and to belong to one another, for the first of a new series, in this Egypt where we have already loved one another so much and possessed one another."

At that moment, the silence was disturbed by the rhythmic throb of an aircraft engine, and in the blue sky a large white bird gilded by the sun passed over the roadster.

Where had that airplane come from? Perhaps from Japan, making a tour of the world, and flying over that millenarian ground: a symbol of progress, the most beautiful effort furnished by the human brain: human wings. Discovery or remembrance? Had not Leonardo da Vinci also attempted the construction of a aircraft?

The travelers watched the great seagull draw away, and, as the Duchess was beginning to be anxious about Adsum's continued silence, she asked him, timidly: "What are you thinking about, Father?"

The old mage turned round toward he young people and enveloped them with a gaze of indulgent generosity. "What am I thinking about, my Daughter? About the Flower of Truth! About the Sun!" He raised his white head toward the dazzling star and said: "Our Father, who art in Heaven..."

Then, lowering his gaze toward Ormus and Diana, he sketched a gesture that might have been a blessing.

"Thy will be done..."

Emotional but untroubled, the lovers lowered their eyes, smiling. There was not only the sky, the soul and survival; there was *us*, the present, desire, the transient moments of a plenitude in which one forgets the world, in which the couple becomes a god holding infinity in the conjugal bond.

The lovers had turned down the lamp of occultism. Her Double was him; his Double, her. Their love killed the ancient world, creating a world of their own.

Adsum turned round again.

Rapidly, they embraced. They summarized their blessings, to the rhythm of the growing light, in a kiss that never ended, into which the dawn, between their ephemeral lips put its eternal roses.

And their hands clasped, in expectation of the evening.

SF & FANTASY

Henri Allorge. *The Great Cataclysm*
Guy d'Armen. *Doc Ardan: The City of Gold and Lepers*
G.-J. Arnaud. *The Ice Company*
Charles Asselineau. *The Double Life*
Cyprien Bérard. *The Vampire Lord Ruthwen*
Aloysius Bertrand. *Gaspard de la Nuit*
Richard Bessière. *The Gardens of the Apocalypse*
Albert Bleunard. *Ever Smaller*
Félix Bodin. *The Novel of the Future*
Alphonse Brown. *City of Glass; The Conquest of the Air*
André Caroff. *The Terror of Madame Atomos; Miss Atomos; The Return of Madame Atomos; The Mistake of Madame Atomos; The Monsters of Madame Atomos; The Revenge of Madame Atomos*
Félicien Champsaur. *The Human Arrow; Ouha, King of the Apes; Pharaoh's Wife*
Didier de Chousy. *Ignis*
Captain Danrit. *Undersea Odyssey*
C. I. Defontenay. *Star (Psi Cassiopeia)*
Charles Derennes. *The People of the Pole*
Georges Dodds (anthologist). *The Missing Link*
Harry Dickson. *The Heir of Dracula*
Jules Dornay. *Lord Ruthven Begins*
Alfred Driou. *The Adventures of a Parisian Aeronaut*
Sâr Dubnotal *vs. Jack the Ripper*
Alexandre Dumas. *The Return of Lord Ruthven*
Renée Dunan. *Baal*
J.-C. Dunyach. *The Night Orchid; The Thieves of Silence*
Henri Duvernois. *The Man Who Found Himself*
Achille Eyraud. *Voyage to Venus*
Henri Falk. *The Age of Lead*
Paul Féval. *Anne of the Isles; Knightshade; Revenants; Vampire City; The Vampire Countess; The Wandering Jew's Daughter*
Paul Féval, *fils. Felifax, the Tiger-Man*
Charles de Fieux. *Lamékis*
Arnould Galopin. *Doctor Omega; Doctor Omega and the Shadowmen*
Judith Gautier. *Isoline and the Serpent-Flower*
Léon Gozlan. *The Vampire of the Val-de-Grâce*

G.L. Gick. *Harry Dickson and the Werewolf of Rutherford Grange*
Edmond Haraucourt. *Illusions of Immortality*
Nathalie Henneberg. *The Green Gods*
V. Hugo, P. Foucher & P. Meurice. *The Hunchback of Notre-Dame*
Romain d'Huissier. *Hexagon: Dark Matter*
Michel Jeury. *Chronolysis*
Gustave Kahn. *The Tale of Gold and Silence*
Gérard Klein. *The Mote in Time's Eye*
Fernand Kolney. *Love in 5000 Years*
Louis-Guillaume de La Follie. *The Unpretentious Philosopher*
Jean de La Hire. *Enter the Nyctalope; The Nyctalope on Mars; The Nyctalope vs. Lucifer; The Nyctalope Steps In; Night of the Nyctalope*
Etienne-Léon de Lamothe-Langon. *The Virgin Vampire*
André Laurie. *Spiridon*
Gabriel de Lautrec. *The Vengeance of the Oval Portrait*
Alain le Drimeur. *The Future City*
Georges Le Faure & Henri de Graffigny. *The Extraordinary Adventures of a Russian Scientist Across the Solar System* (2 vols.)
Gustave Le Rouge. *The Vampires of Mars; The Dominion of the World* (w/Gustave Guitton) (4 vols.)
Jules Lermina. *Mysteryville; Panic in Paris; To-Ho and the Gold Destroyers; The Secret of Zippelius*
Jean-Marc & Randy Lofficier. *Edgar Allan Poe on Mars; The Katrina Protocol; Pacifica; Robonocchio; Tales of the Shadowmen 1-9*
Xavier Mauméjean. *The League of Heroes*
Joseph Méry. *The Tower of Destiny*
Hippolyte Mettais. *The Year 5865*
Louise Michel. *The Human Microbes; The New World*
José Moselli. *Illa's End*
John-Antoine Nau. *Enemy Force*
Marie Nizet. *Captain Vampire*
C. Nodier, A. Beraud & Toussaint-Merle. *Frankenstein*
Henri de Parville. *An Inhabitant of the Planet Mars*
Gaston de Pawlowski. *Journey to the Land of the 4th Dimension*
Georges Pellerin. *The World in 2000 Years*
Ernest Pérochon. *The Frenetic People*
Pierre Pelot. *The Child Who Walked on the Sky*
J. Polidori, C. Nodier, E. Scribe. *Lord Ruthven the Vampire*
P.-A. Ponson du Terrail. *The Vampire and the Devil's Son*
Henri de Régnier. *A Surfeit of Mirrors*

Maurice Renard. *The Blue Peril; Doctor Lerne; The Doctored Man; A Man Among the Microbes; The Master of Light*
Jean Richepin. *The Wing; The Crazy Corner*
Albert Robida. *The Adventures of Saturnin Farandoul; The Clock of the Centuries; Chalet in the Sky*
J.-H. Rosny Aîné. *Helgvor of the Blue River; The Givreuse Enigma; The Mysterious Force; The Navigators of Space; Vamireh; The World of the Variants; The Young Vampire*
Marcel Rouff. *Journey to the Inverted World*
Han Ryner. *The Superhumans*
Brian Stableford. *The New Faust at the Tragicomique; The Empire of the Necromancers (The Shadow of Frankenstein; Frankenstein and the Vampire Countess; Frankenstein in London); Sherlock Holmes & The Vampires of Eternity; The Stones of Camelot; The Wayward Muse.* (anthologist) *The Germans on Venus; News from the Moon; The Supreme Progress; The World Above the World; Nemoville; Investigations of the Future*
Jacques Spitz. *The Eye of Purgatory*
Kurt Steiner. *Ortog*
Eugène Thébault. *Radio-Terror*
C.-F. Tiphaigne de La Roche. *Amilec*
Théo Varlet. *The Golden Rock. The Xenobiotic Invasion; Timeslip Troopers* (w/André Blandin); *The Martian Epic* (w/Octave Joncquel)
Paul Vibert. *The Mysterious Fluid*
Villiers de l'Isle-Adam. *The Scaffold; The Vampire Soul*
Philippe Ward. *Artahe*
Philippe Ward & Sylvie Miller. *The Song of Montségur*

MYSTERIES & THRILLERS

M. Allain & P. Souvestre. *The Daughter of Fantômas*
A. Anicet-Bourgeois, Lucien Dabril. *Rocambole*
A. Bernède. *Belphegor*; *Judex* (w/Louis Feuillade)
A. Bisson & G. Livet. *Nick Carter vs. Fantômas*
V. Darlay & H. de Gorsse. *Arsène Lupin vs. Sherlock Holmes: The Stage Play*
Séamas Duffy. *Sherlock Holmes in Paris*
Paul Féval. *Gentlemen of the Night; John Devil; The Black Coats ('Salem Street; The Invisible Weapon; The Parisian Jungle; The Companions of the Treasure; Heart of Steel; The Cadet Gang; The Sword-Swallower)*

Emile Gaboriau. *Monsieur Lecoq*
Goron & Emile Gautier. *Spawn of the Penitentiary*
Steve Leadley. *Sherlock Holmes: The Circle of Blood*
Maurice Leblanc. *Arsène Lupin vs. Countess Cagliostro; Arsène Lupin vs. Sherlock Holmes (The Blonde Phantom; The Hollow Needle); The Many Faces of Arsène Lupin*
Gaston Leroux. *Chéri-Bibi; The Phantom of the Opera; Rouletabille & the Mystery of the Yellow Room; Rouletabille at Krupp's*
Richard Marsh. *The Complete Adventures of Judith Lee*
William Patrick Maynard. *The Terror of Fu Manchu; The Destiny of Fu Manchu*
Frank J. Morlock. *Sherlock Holmes: The Grand Horizontals; Sherlock Holmes vs Jack the Ripper*
Antonin Reschal. *The Adventures of Miss Boston*
P. de Wattyne & Y. Walter. *Sherlock Holmes vs. Fantômas*
David White. *Fantômas in America*

SCREENPLAYS

Mike Baron. *The Iron Triangle*
Emma Bull & Will Shetterly. *Nightspeeder; War for the Oaks*
Gerry Conway & Roy Thomas. *Doc Dynamo*
Steve Englehart. *Majorca*
James Hudnall. *The Devastator*
Jean-Marc & Randy Lofficier. *Royal Flush*
J.-M. & R. Lofficier & Marc Agapit. *Despair*
J.-M. & R. Lofficier & Joël Houssin. *City*
Andrew Paquette. *Peripheral Vision*
Robert L. Robinson, Jr. *Judex*
R. Thomas, J. Hendler & L. Sprague de Camp. *Rivers of Time*

NON-FICTION

Stephen R. Bissette. *Blur 1-5. Green Mountain Cinema 1; Teen Angels*
Win Scott Eckert. *Crossovers* (2 vols.)
Jean-Marc & Randy Lofficier. *Shadowmen* (2 vols.)
Randy Lofficier. *Over Here*

www.ingramcontent.com/pod-product-compliance
Lightning Source LLC
Chambersburg PA
CBHW060354030726
47497CB00003B/709